From the Chicken House

Don't you just love a really dangerous mystery? One in which there are shady lords, faded film stars, horrible gangsters, and brave kids who take on the impossible to unravel deeply perilous secrets of the past? Well, this funny, fast and furious story by Sam Hepburn is what you and I have been waiting for! I can tell you who . . . urgghh . . . no, too late, urghhh . . . read the book!

Barry Cunningham
Publisher

CHASING THE DARK

SAM HEPBURN

Chicken House

2 Palmer Street, Frome, Somerset BA11 1DS

Text © Sam Hepburn 2013
First published in Great Britain in 2013
The Chicken House
2 Palmer Street
Frome, Somerset BA11 1DS
United Kingdom
www.doublecluck.com

Cover design and interior design by Mavro Design
Typeset by Dorchester Typesetting Group Ltd
Printed and bound in Great Britain by CPI Group (UK) Ltd, Croydon, CR0 4YY
The paper used in this Chicken House book is made from wood grown in sustainable
forests.

1 3 5 7 9 10 8 6 4 2

British Library Cataloguing in Publication data available.

ISBN 978-1-908435-68-2

For Bodour *Abu Affan* and Fareed *Atabani*, with love

CHAPTER 1

Dark night. Rain-slashed road. A great black 4x4 screeching out of nowhere, its headlights catching Mum's pale, frightened face behind the windscreen of a tinny little hatchback. She's screaming into the brightness, throwing up her arms . . .

The sick smash of metal jerked me awake.

I pushed my head into the pillow, clinging to the split second of possibility that Mum was alive, that I was home in my own bed and the crash was just some hi-def, surround-sound nightmare, brought on by a late-night movie. I strained for the sound of Mum's voice calling me to get up. The silence got bigger, pressing me down.

I couldn't breathe. Slowly, I turned my head and opened my eyes.

The sight of my Aunt Doreen's spotless spare room hit

me so hard I had to bunch up my knees and grip the mattress to fight the pain. It took a while before I got it together enough to try anything normal like pulling on yesterday's clothes, dragging myself downstairs or tuning in to the conversation going on in the kitchen.

' . . . she won't have left him a penny. You realise that, don't you, George? Heaven knows what it's going to cost us to feed him, let alone clothe him. When he walked into that church I was so ashamed I wanted the earth to swallow me up. Jeans and trainers! At his own mother's funeral!'

Doreen's voice was shrill and fluttery like one of next door's chickens and if she was turning up the volume to make sure I heard her, she needn't have bothered. I already knew I was about as welcome in my aunt's life as a cockroach on one of her fancy cupcakes. So I just sat on the stairs, pretending I was listening to an actress in one of the soaps moaning about a kid who wasn't real. A kid who wasn't me. I'd been doing that a lot lately because right now being Joe Slattery was crap.

'Come on, love, he's had a tough time . . .' Her husband, George, was talking slowly and carefully, as if he was checking the wires on a ticking bomb, wondering which one to snip. 'We owe it to your sister to do our best for him.'

Bad move, George. The explosion was delayed by a horrible silence while Doreen sucked air, the way little kids do before they start yelling.

'And what did my *sister* ever do for me? Nothing! She just went her own selfish, irresponsible way and expected everyone else to pick up the pieces. Landing us with her slum kid. It's not right, George. And it's not fair. Where's the father? That's what I want to know.'

My fingers itched to hit the remote and switch Doreen off.

'He seems a nice enough lad and as soon as they find him a school he'll be out of your hair.'

'How long's that going to take? He'll be mooning round the house for weeks trying to smuggle that disgusting dog inside. He's lucky I'm letting him keep it at all.'

'I know, love. You've been great about it.'

I left them to it and crept outside. As I eased the door shut, my dog Oz stopped digging up the flowerbed and hurtled across the lawn, nearly choking himself on the long, clanking chain Doreen had got him tied to. Calling him disgusting was pretty harsh, but even I had to admit that he was a bit deficient in the cute looks and winning ways department. Mum had reckoned he was mostly Yorkie, with a bit of bull terrier thrown in, on account of his stocky shoulders and squashed-up face. He had a wild look in his squinty black eyes, a greyish-white coat that felt like wire, and this lumpy bald patch down one side where the fur refused to grow back over a couple of scars he'd got fighting. Still, looks aren't everything. And it wasn't his fault he'd puked on Doreen's carpet. He's not used to long car journeys. But what with that and the fact that she and Mum had always hated each other's guts, you could kind of see why Doreen had had it in for us right from the start.

Oz was straining towards the back door, tongue hanging out.

'Forget it,' I said. 'You've got no chance. Come on.'

I raced him down to the shed he was sleeping in. It didn't look so bad. George had got him a sack of dog biscuits, and I'd made him a bed from some old clothes Doreen had put out for the jumble. I got to thinking it'd probably be easier all round if I just moved in here, too. I unclipped his chain and chucked a handful of biscuits in his bowl.

While he bolted them down, I stared at Doreen and George's house through the shed window. Funny to think that it was where Mum had grown up. I could just about remember her bringing me here to visit her parents, but they died when I was a kid – Grandad first, then Nan a couple of years later. Mum and Doreen had practically stopped speaking by then and once Mum had sold Doreen her share of Laurel Cottage, she'd never set foot in Saxted again. Mum used the money to buy a flat in North London. Only Mum being Mum, she fell behind with the mortgage and it got repossessed.

After that things went downhill pretty fast. Rented flats, shared houses, bedsits, till we hit an all-time low and ended up on the Farm Street Estate. That was around the time she met that creep Eddy Fletcher. He said he'd got contacts in the music business and could get her a recording contract. Turned out he was a dodgy electrician who'd once done three weeks as a roadie and never got over it. As soon as he moved in he decided to ease up on work so he could devote more time to making Mum's life a misery.

Just thinking about him made my fists clench up and my breath go shaky. But before I started smashing up

George's flowerpots, Oz threw himself at me, desperate for a walk. I let him out the back gate, pounded after him and stood panting at the end of the lane, trying to decide whether to turn right towards Saxted station or left towards the swanky new estate. I didn't do either. I went straight on to the churchyard, which was pretty stupid seeing as how I was trying not to think about Mum. My feet had obviously missed the all-out ban on that one.

Oz raced ahead and I could see he was torn about his new life. Something in his little doggy brain was telling him that fields and fresh air were a good thing, but he was having trouble squaring that with living in the shed and being chained up 24/7. Me, I couldn't be bothered to decide either way about country life because I knew Doreen wasn't going to put up with having a 'slum kid' around for one nanosecond longer than she could help. Who knew where I'd be by next week? I'll say one thing for her, though, I don't think she gave a stuff about my dad being Kenyan. As far as Doreen was concerned, this was personal.

Mum's grave was right there, by the churchyard fence, just a mound of earth and a pile of wet, muddy wreaths. No gravestone yet or probably ever, 'cos I couldn't see that tightwad Eddy forking out for one and I hadn't noticed Doreen offering to sort it.

'Course, even yesterday at the funeral Eddy wouldn't let it drop about the bloke who'd been giving Mum a lift. *Who was he? What was she doing with him?* As if the police hadn't told us who he was – some poncey journalist called Ivo Lincoln. This tall posh bloke with a droopy face came up

5

to me at the hospital and said he was Lincoln's dad and he was sorry for my loss and I said I was sorry for his, but it was just words. The cops said the crash wasn't Lincoln's fault, that he was well under the limit and it was all down to the maniac in the 4x4. But if Lincoln hadn't been there, hadn't existed, it wouldn't have happened. What was anyone with a name like Ivo doing in a dump like the Trafalgar Arms anyway? All the pubs round our way were rough, but the Trafalgar Arms was the worst. It wasn't fair that Mum had ended up doing gigs in a place like that, not when you think of all the dreams she'd had. Though I like to think she'd had her moments. There was the summer we lived in a mini-van and she got to sing at a big festival in Cornwall, and the time one of her tapes got played on Radio Two.

My eyes were welling up so I made a dash for the woods down the side of the churchyard. Oz went mad, jabbing his nose into every bush he passed before catching a sniff of squirrel and chasing it down an overgrown track between the trees. I figured he wasn't used to things that smelled good having legs. I stumbled after him, dodging mud holes, tripping over tree roots and pushing away branches that kept twanging back in my eyes. By the time I caught up with him he'd given up on the wildlife and started peeing against a pile of car tyres ditched beside an old mattress. It probably made him feel at home. You see, the first time I ever saw him he was down by the council dump fighting an Alsatian twice his size. The Alsatian won and Oz was in such a bad way I took him home. Eddy kicked off about it but Mum said it made her feel safer having a dog around … and now I was back to thinking about Mum. I walked on, swishing a stick. Sometimes it helped if I kept moving.

I'd been going a while, trying to find something to think about that didn't involve death or Doreen, when I got to a high brick wall overgrown with creepers and topped by a row of deadly-looking spikes. I followed it round till I came to a huge boarded-up gateway, the kind that didn't need the 'Keep Out, Trespassers Will Be Prosecuted' signs stuck all over it to give you the hint that visitors weren't welcome. Now I'm not the rugged, outdoorsy type – more the weedy, indoorsy type and small for fourteen. But I am pretty nosy, and seeing as my schedule that morning wasn't exactly hectic, I hauled myself up this big tree, wriggled down an overhanging branch and took a peek over the wall.

You should have seen the house on the other side. Crumbling old mansion? Forget it. This place was all jagged layers of glass and wood laid out in a massive L-shape. The curtains were closed, which made the whole house look like it was asleep and hadn't noticed the moss growing over the terrace, the rotten leaves swirling round the empty swimming pool, or the row of dead palm trees that led to a big conservatory with bits of awning flapping round the doors. The garden stretched on forever but apart from a sorry-looking tennis court and a big smashed-up greenhouse it was so overgrown that all you could see was weeds, fallen trees and a few ivy-covered statues poking through the brambles.

The statue nearest the greenhouse was a half-naked,

one-armed woman and I swear something was moving in the bushes round her feet. I leant closer, trying to get a better look, and nearly fell off when Oz came scrabbling out, shaking mud off his fur.

'Get out of there!' I yelled. 'Right now!'

He ran up and down for a bit barking at the wall then gave up and started giving me dirty looks like it was my fault he was trapped. I couldn't just leave him there so I wriggled down the branch, clung on to the bendy bit hanging over the wall, shut my eyes and lowered myself into the garden. Well, when I say lowered I mean half fell, half slithered, ripping the skin of both hands, and twisting my ankle as I hit the ground. But the strange thrill I got from being inside those walls kind of cancelled out the pain. Oz kept close as I fought my way through the brambles, hobbled up the terrace steps, stuck my nose against the French windows and squinted through a gap in the curtains.

A thin wedge of daylight slashed the darkness inside, lighting up a poster-sized photo of a woman. She was what Mum would have called 'striking'. Kind of beautiful but deathly pale with weird, slanty eyes that were nearly too big for her face, eyelashes as thick as tarantulas' legs and dark brown hair piled up high on her head. She was looking straight at me over her shoulder as if she knew me or something. I stared back for a long time like maybe I knew her too, but when I blinked, my brain flashed up Eddy Fletcher swiping the photo of Mum off our sideboard and yelling that she was a dirty, two-timing . . .

A deafening crash shut him up. I'd kicked the French

8

window so hard my foot had smashed right through the glass. I whipped round, petrified someone had heard. I waited. Nothing. No shouts. No footsteps. Just the panicky rattle of my own breath. I leant against the wall, trying to get up the nerve to run or go inside. Next thing I knew I was kicking out a hole big enough to squeeze through, lifting Oz carefully over the broken glass, and crawling in.

The long dining table, the chunky candlesticks, the half-burnt log in the fireplace, even the cobwebs were covered in a furry fuzz of dust. Two huge chandeliers made of tiny bubbles of glass hovered over the table like giant jellyfish, and when I tapped one of them the hollow ringing sound made the fuzz twitch like I'd woken a ghost.

I backed out of there. Oz's claws clicked on the wooden floor as he followed me past a pair of double doors, through a wide hallway, past a spiral staircase and into a massive room full of spooky shapes draped in white sheets. I drifted around, lifting them up and peering underneath. A wood-panelled bar, a white grand piano, a glass coffee table, three long leather couches. There were loads more photos of the same woman staring through the cobwebs; pictures of her prancing about in miniskirts, trying on hats, cupping her face in her hands, and one of her wearing a floaty white dress, holding up a wine glass and laughing. It was like she was everywhere, watching every move I made. Oz padded over and sniffed at a picture frame lying face down on the floor by the window. I bent down and turned it over. The woman's slanty eyes stared back at me through a layer of shattered glass. I picked off the splinters and read the words scrawled in the corner: *To Harry, A star in the making. Best wishes always. N.C. xxx.*

Oz barked. The curtain moved. As I spun round, a huge claw yanked me off my feet, ripping terror through my guts. The knife pricking my throat cut off my scream. A pair of black, bloodshot eyes glared down at me out of a filthy, sunken face. This guy was old but he was tall and strong. His head was shaved like a wrinkly nut, there was a scar running from his left eye to his cheek, and he smelled like rotting meat. A swift jab from his boot sent Oz slithering into a growling, quivery crouch.

'What you do here?' His voice was foreign and his Ws came out like Vs.

'I . . . nothing.' I could hardly spit out the words.

'Who with you?'

'No one … honest.'

'What your name?'

'J . . . Joe. I wasn't going to nick anything.'

'Joe, who?'

'S . . . Slattery.'

'Where you live?'

'L . . . Laurel Cottage.'

I should have lied but fear had cut the connection between my mouth and brain.

He lowered the knife. 'Empty your pockets.'

I shook out about fifty pence in coins, a square of gum and my phone. It was a cheap old Nokia I'd got from my mate Bailey, but handing it over really hacked me off. He threw me back against the wall. Struggling to breathe I snatched another glance at him. He was a tramp. Filthy, stinking, and old enough to be my grandad. Bailey was going to wet himself when I told him I'd been mugged by an OAP.

He pulled back a tear in the leg of his filthy trousers. I looked where he was pointing. A deep gash ran from his knee to his boot, oozing a mess of blood and pus that had gone crusty round a strip of white that had to be bone.

'You help me,' he said. It wasn't a request.

I stared at the wound, trying not to puke.

He made a jab at me with the knife.

'OK.' I raised my hands. 'I'll r . . . ring . . . for a doctor.'

'No doctor! Get bandage, medicine, food, money.'

'I can't . . . I . . . I live with my aunt . . . she won't let me touch her stuff.'

He wasn't up for a cosy chat about the tough time I was having at Doreen's and just rattled out the list again. 'Bandage. Medicine. Food. Money.'

'OK, OK, I'll ... I'll do my best.' I scraped myself off the wall and edged towards the door. 'Come on, Oz.'

With a low grunt, the tramp grabbed Oz by the scruff of his neck and waved the knife at his throat. Oz was so surprised he just hung there with his eyes popping out of his head.

'Go. You come back tonight or I kill dog.'

'What?' He was crazy. 'Let him go! I swear I'll come back.'

He jerked the knife under Oz's collar.

'All right! I'll get the stuff. Just don't hurt him.'

Oz gave me this look like I'd got to be joking, as I left him dangling and kept walking.

I stopped. My voice came out in a whimper. 'I can't get over the wall.'

The tramp slipped the knife between his teeth and chucked me a bunch of keys.

'Door. By greenhouse.'

He lifted Oz higher and prodded his stomach, like some deranged TV cook testing a Christmas turkey. 'You don't bring back keys, I kill dog. You bring police, I kill dog. You tell anyone I here, I come *Laurel Cottage* and I kill you, Joe Slattery.'

CHAPTER 2

I stumbled across the garden, slipping and shaking so much I dropped the keys and had to scrabble in the mud to find them. Crashing through the brambles, I scanned the wall and spotted a little wooden door. It was half hidden behind the greenhouse and its paintwork was all blistered and peeling off in strips. Pushing towards it, I tripped and fell against the one-armed statue I'd seen from the tree. Her blank marble eyes stared straight through me. I dodged past her and fumbled for the likeliest key, turned it in the keyhole and lurched into the woods, trying not to look at the empty space beside me where Oz should have been.

Thankfully George was in the lounge reading the paper and Doreen was clattering about in the kitchen, listening to the radio. I kicked off my trainers and crept up to my room, which was all done out in cream and white and about as welcoming as a dentist's surgery. Till then I'd hardly dared set foot in the gleaming en suite bathroom but I tore off my muddy clothes, ran for the shower and let the boiling water pound my face while I tried to work out the chances of getting Oz back alive, why that crazy old tramp didn't want a doctor, and how come he'd got the keys to that house. According to some test we'd done at school my IQ was up there with the geeks but I couldn't even take a guess at the answers.

I pulled on a pair of track pants and a T-shirt, listening to Doreen having a go at George about money. He had his own engineering works but it sounded like business had taken a nose-dive and Doreen wasn't happy about it, 'specially now they had 'that slum kid sucking them dry'. I switched channels – back to the horror show playing in that abandoned house – and tried to stop panicking about what I should do. It was a no-brainer. Keep my mouth shut, get the tramp the stuff he wanted and save Oz. I ran through the things he'd asked for. Bandages and medicine – there was sure to be something in the house. Food – Doreen might not miss that, she had cupboards full of it. Cash – not so easy. This was a nightmare. The minute Doreen found out I was a thief she'd chuck me out. But I couldn't let Oz down. Not now, not ever. He was all I'd got.

When George called me down to eat I mumbled something about cutting myself on some barbed wire and asked if they'd got a first-aid kit. Doreen pointed to the cupboard under the sink. I sorted myself a plaster and gave a mental thumbs-up when I saw all the bandages, antiseptic creams and packets of gauze.

Weighed down by what I was planning, I sat at the table watching Doreen dish up some strange-looking stew that had dark slimy things floating round with the meat. When I asked what they were she said they were prunes. Weird. She'd got her own catering company, making dinners for people who wanted to impress their bosses without getting their hands dirty, and it looked like we were getting the leftovers from some client's party. Still, anything was better than cold baked beans out of the tin, which is what I'd been living on since Mum died. My eyes flicked to the extension off the kitchen which was fitted out with fridges, freezers and stainless steel units stacked with all Doreen's catering stuff. I wasn't supposed to go in there and as for Oz . . . well, I won't mention what Doreen said she'd do to him if he even took a sniff in that direction.

Mum said her relationship with Doreen had always been tricky but it crashed and burned when Mum went and called her a neurotic, stuck-up, pain in the neck. Spot on, if you ask me. But if you're singing at your sister's wedding there's probably some musicians' law that says you're s'posed to turn the microphone off before you start slagging off the bride. Mum was sorry afterwards and said she'd only done it because she'd had a bit too much to drink. Trouble was, Mum had done a lot of stupid things because she'd had a bit too much to drink, like cadging that lift home from the Trafalgar Arms with some bloke she didn't even know and getting smashed up in a car crash. Don't get me wrong, I loved my mum and she loved me, and just thinking about her is like getting tasered and thrown against an electric fence. But what with the problems with Eddy, the money worries and her getting so depressed all the time, I'd been scared for a while that something bad might happen to her. And then it did.

George was doing his best, piling veg on my plate and asking if I was musical like Mum and what my favourite subjects were at school. But Doreen tapping her nails on her wine glass and giving me the evil eye didn't exactly help to keep the chit-chat flowing. You'd never think she was Mum's sister, not in a million years. I mean, Doreen was fair where Mum had been dark and she was bony where Mum had been what she called 'curvy', and she had a hard pointy face and small blue-ish eyes, whereas Mum's face had been soft and pretty and her big dark eyes had been her best feature. Doreen also had tiny lines round her mouth that got deeper whenever she looked at me.

George was a big bloke, ex-Royal Engineers, but one squawk from Doreen and he turned into a total wuss. He even called her Dilly – which made me want to puke. Though to be fair, I didn't rate his chances if he ever crossed her. He didn't seem to notice he'd married a harpy and he spent most of his time gazing at her as if he couldn't believe his luck. But he was looking at me now, telling me he'd be going to Germany soon to pitch for some big contract and he was glad Doreen would have me for company while he was away. You should have seen the look she gave him.

Guess what, Doreen? Being stuck with you isn't top of my wish list either.

Still, at least while I was here no one was going to be asking me if I wanted to 'talk about it'. 'Course I didn't. What was there to say? Mum was dead. End of.

I offered to wash up. Doreen wasn't keen; she said she liked things done properly. I went upstairs, wondering how I was going to kill the time till she and George went to bed. I didn't have a computer – or even a phone now the tramp had taken mine. Not that I was in the mood for playing games, what with Oz staring death in the eye and Mum . . . well, you know.

I was sitting on the bed picking at a hole in my sock when George tapped on the door and came in with a box of books.

'I found a few of my old favourites in the attic,' he said, dumping the box on the duvet. 'I think there's some of your aunt's in here, too.' He sat down awkwardly. 'She doesn't mean it, you know. She's just highly strung. Underneath she's got a heart of gold.'

Whatever hard metallic substance Doreen's heart was made of, it definitely wasn't gold.

'She's just taking a while to adjust to having a young-ster around the place.'

I nodded and started checking out the books: *Biggles Learns to Fly,* the *Guinness Book of Records* for 1972, a torn copy of something called *Kidnapped* and a load of *Jackie* annuals with dorky-looking girls on the front. I gave up when I got to a layer of recipe books and knitting patterns and flipped open *Kidnapped*. Under the Park Hill School crest someone had written 'Awarded to Sadie Slattery for punctual attendance at choir practice'. My eyes blurred up. George looked embarrassed, gave me this awkward pat with his big, sausagey fingers, and made for the door. 'You'll be OK, Joe. Just give it time.'

Yeah, right.

I gave it twenty minutes after George had gone before slipping out to the shed pretending I was going to see Oz. Edging round his empty bed, I stuffed my pockets with dog biscuits and hunted round for a torch. George caught me coming back indoors and looked dead guilty when I headed straight for my room, though he cheered up when I told him I was getting stuck into *Kidnapped*.

Actually, it was pretty good – all about this orphan, David Balfour, who gets abducted by his evil Uncle Ebenezer. But I was too terrified to concentrate on David Balfour's problems; terrified of what that old tramp might do to Oz and terrified that Doreen was going to catch me nicking her stuff. I was quaking so much I waited another hour after she and George had gone to bed before I even dared open my door.

Every step creaked, every hinge screeched. I couldn't believe she didn't come running. I grabbed what I needed from the first-aid kit plus a couple of apples, a packet of biscuits and half a loaf from the kitchen before I went for Doreen's catering supplies, reckoning she'd take longer to notice they'd been raided. I stuffed a whole salami and a jar of olives into a plastic carrier, sliced a lump off a big pink ham covered in herbs and another from a crumbly wedge of cheese, and added them to my stash. I hesitated, not sure how much stuff I'd need to buy Oz's freedom. Just to be on the safe side I snatched a bottle of brandy, a bar of dark chocolate and a box of macaroons, and shoved the lot in my backpack. George's jacket was hanging in the hall. Feeling sick, I felt around for his wallet. There was seventy quid in there. I took forty. *Sorry, George. Really, really I am.*

The track through the woods had been tough going in daylight, but it was a million times worse at night and a feeble torch beam wasn't much help against a mass of foot-grabbing, eye-gouging trees. As for the noises, I don't know which were scarier – the twigs that kept snapping like someone was following me, or the sudden bursts of rustling that turned into muttering as I blundered past. I kept close to the brick wall, following it round. Even then I nearly missed the door. I was juggling the torch and the keys, looking for the right one, when I noticed the key ring had a crest on it. It was two bears standing on their back legs holding up a shield. Something creaked in the trees, stirring the leaves. Checking over my shoulder, I unlocked the door, and stumbled into the garden.

The tramp was waiting as I crawled in through the hole in the French windows. He didn't look any friendlier by torchlight and neither did his knife. He snatched the torch, switched it off and shoved it in my back, nudging me across the dining room, through the moonlit hall and down a pitch-black corridor. I heard a scrape of wood, and the darkness took on a flickery tinge of gold. I took a step nearer and looked down a rickety staircase into a brick-walled cellar.

I'd seen enough detective shows to know that a cellar, a kid and a crazy old tramp were a bad combination and that sometimes it could take the rest of the world ten or twenty years to find out just how bad. I heard a yelp. It was Oz. At least we were going to die together.

'Move,' ordered the tramp.

I wasn't going to argue.

It was cold and smelly down there but he'd got candles going, and brought down a mattress and blankets. Although Oz was tied up, the rope was long and, judging by the white hairs all over the blankets, he'd been making himself comfortable. He jumped up at me and I held him tight, letting him lick my face while the tramp tipped up my backpack and started prodding everything I'd brought him with his knife. Oz leapt out of my arms and made a dash for the ham. The tramp snarled. I grabbed Oz back and shoved a handful of dog biscuits under his nose.

'You are good boy,' the tramp said, raising the bottle of brandy at me and biting a lump of salami off the end of his knife.

You are crazy maniac, I thought.

He tossed Oz a bit of salami. My eyes were getting used to the gloom and I had a look around, taking in a huge boiler, lines of pipes and cables running everywhere, and a rack of dusty tools hung above a workbench. The tramp had been busy. He'd cleaned up a hammer, a wrench and a screwdriver, and laid them out on the bench next to a rusty tin box roughly the size of a brick. Through smears of mud I made out the word OXO printed on the lid in fat white letters. He caught me staring at it. I turned away quick. When I looked back he'd slipped it out of sight.

'You help me,' he said, pulling his ripped trouser leg up to his thigh. Just looking at that pus-crusted scab and the blue-white bone made me want to throw up.

'I . . . I can't. I don't know how.'

'Kitchen. Hot water.' He tossed me a cigarette lighter and started gulping down the brandy like it was Coke.

I fumbled my way upstairs, waving the tiny flame through the dark till I found the kitchen. The slatted blind was throwing lines of watery moonlight across a sink, a cooker, miles of black and white floor, a long breakfast bar and walls of cupboards. Everything in there was draped in cobwebs, right down to the withered piece of soap on the draining board.

I filled the kettle and put it on to boil. The tramp had obviously been using those tools in the cellar to turn on the gas and water. Maybe tricks like that came easy if you spent your life breaking into empty houses. I turned the lighter over in my hand. It looked like it was gold and the shimmering gas flame lit up a swirly engraving on the side. Classy. Where'd he nicked that from?

Leaving the water to heat up, I searched for a bowl, flickering the lighter into drawers and cupboards full of pots, pans, knives, forks, tin openers, fancy china – everything you could think of. It was like the owner had just nipped out, meaning to come back. That's how our flat had looked after Mum died. All her stuff still sitting there, just the way she'd left it. I grabbed a mixing bowl, picked up the kettle and stumbled back to the cellar.

Most of the brandy had gone but this guy wasn't even tipsy. He took off his belt, bit down on the leather, and growled at me to get on with it. I pulled off his boot and felt the puke rise. It wasn't just the stink making me retch. His foot was like something out of a joke shop: three cracked yellow claws sticking out of a rubbery lump of grey flesh, scabbed all over with red puffy sores. I didn't want to know what had happened to the rest of his toes and I don't even want to think about what I did next.

But after about half an hour there was an oily black scum speckled with bits of gravel and grass floating in the bowl and I'd squeezed half a tube of antiseptic on to his leg, bandaging it up as tight as I could. It must have hurt like hell, though he never flinched once. I handed him a couple of aspirin, which he washed down with the last of the brandy.

'You come tomorrow night,' he said.

If Doreen found out I'd been stealing I probably wouldn't even *be* in Saxted by tomorrow night, and no way was I leaving without Oz.

'OK,' I said. 'But I want my dog.'

He shook his head and patted Oz's head.

'You come back, Joe Slattery. Or I eat him.' A black hole fringed with stumpy brown teeth opened in his face.

The effect was so horrible it took me a while to realise he was smiling.

CHAPTER 3

The gut-twisting crunch of the 4x4 slamming into Lincoln's car was getting to be my morning wake-up call. As usual, the nightmare left me sweaty and trembling.

Slowly I pulled on some clothes and looked out the window. Doreen's car had gone and I knew George would be at work. Relieved to be on my own, I went downstairs. I wasn't hungry but I wandered round the kitchen like a broken robot, burning toast, spilling juice, dropping knives. As soon as I stopped the house went completely silent, unlike the inside of my head, which was about as quiet as the time they let a student teacher take our maths class. Thoughts whizzed about like paper aeroplanes and just about everyone I wanted to forget was in there, getting rowdier by the minute: Doreen calling me a slum kid; Eddy accusing Mum of having an affair; the vicar droning on and on about dust and ashes; the cops telling me they still hadn't found the driver who'd killed Mum. What were they playing at? The CCTV had caught the black 4x4 swerving on to the wrong side of the road, smashing straight into Lincoln's car then rocketing away, but they said the cameras had lost track of it somewhere round Dalston. OK, so the number plate had been too muddy to make out but huge, great 4x4s with bashed-up bonnets don't just disappear, even in Dalston.

I dragged my thoughts away from the crash and tried to focus on the wounded tramp rotting away in that abandoned house. It was like both of us were hanging on to our rubbish lives by a couple of threads, and any second now they'd snap and we'd both go plunging over the edge. What I needed was Mum back. What he needed was antibiotics.

I rushed up to George and Doreen's gleaming bathroom and poked around their medicine cabinet, pouncing on a packet of tablets that said antibiotic on the label. Just as I grabbed a bottle of extra-strength painkillers I heard Doreen's car pulling into the drive. I've never moved so fast in my life, shoving the rest of the stuff back, straightening the towels, rubbing greasy finger marks off the mirror. I just made it down to the hall as she came in, lugging a bag of shopping.

She looked at me suspiciously. 'What were you doing?'

'I was . . . just going to clear my breakfast away. Then I'm going to take Oz for a walk.'

She sniffed. 'You and I need to get a couple of things straight, young man. I've got a business to run. I'm in and out the whole time sourcing ingredients, making deliveries, meeting clients. You can't expect me to keep running back to the house to let you in every time you take that dog out.'

'I know, it's just that he needs . . .'

'Quite against my better judgement, George has persuaded me to give you this.' She got a key out of her bag and handed it to me. 'It's for the back door. Use it. If you *ever* go out and forget to lock up there'll be trouble. Do you hear me?'

'Yes.' I slipped the key in my pocket. 'I won't forget, I promise.'

I could see she wasn't convinced but actually my memory is pretty good, which is tough considering the amount of stuff I'd rather forget. I don't know where I get it from. Not Mum, that's for sure, and certainly not my dad. His memory was so bad he went home to see them and forgot to come back.

Doreen shrugged off her coat, tutting when the doorbell chimed. She pulled it open.

There were two cops on the doorstep asking for me. Doreen chivvied them inside, probably hoping I'd been seen vandalising the bus stop. But I could tell it was something to do with Mum. They were both doing the same twitchy, puffed-up thing with their cheeks that WPC *please call me Lauren* Burnett had been doing when she sat on our couch and broke the news about Mum being in a car crash. Too numb to speak I'd just kept looking into Lauren's round blue eyes, wishing she'd start blinking and stop squeezing my arm. The young cop who came with her had stood there staring at the floor all pink in the face, edging his cap round and round in his hands while Eddy ranted and raved about Mum being in another man's car.

'You all right, lad?' The taller cop was leaning forward, peering at me.

My heart was pumping. 'Have you caught the hit-and-run driver who killed my mother?'

His cheeks got twitchier. 'You'll have to talk to the Met about the investigation. We're Kent victim support.' He handed me a leaflet.

'So what is this about, officer?' Doreen said.

'Forensics have finished with the vehicle and released Miss Slattery's effects.' He tipped his head towards the cardboard box his partner was holding and handed me an electronic message pad. 'We . . . need a signature. Just a formality.'

I scribbled on the screen and reached for the box. Surprised by the weight, I nearly dropped it.

They turned to go. 'Any questions, give the number on that leaflet a call,' said the shorter cop.

'Right,' I said.

Doreen closed the door, eyeing the box. Before she could say a word I made a dash for my room, kicked the door shut and laid the box on the bed. I must have sat there looking at it for at least half an hour. Stupid really. The worst thing I could ever imagine had already happened to me and I was getting spooked by a cardboard box. Forcing myself, I stretched out a fingertip, nudged up the lid and sneaked a look.

If I hadn't been so angry I'd have laughed. No wonder the cops couldn't find the hit-and-run driver. They couldn't even get the right 'effects' back to the right family. Inside was a holdall, but it wasn't Mum's. I lifted it out. A jab of misery snuffed out the fury. Mum's bag, the black squishy one she carried all the time, was lying underneath it. Tugging back the zipper, I caught the faint, familiar smell of her, which got stronger as I took her things out one by one. Her empty purse, a trashy romance called *Love Me Do*, a biro, a make-up bag bursting with little tubes and brushes, a bottle of her perfume and a crumpled tissue with a lip-shaped smudge of lipstick in the corner. Just for a second I pretended she was standing behind me and when I turned round she'd be tying her hair back or buttoning her coat and telling me not to mess with her things.

The silence in that room was crushing my lungs. I threw open the window, and stuck my head out, gulping air, trying to get a grip. But my hands were still trembling as I scooped Mum's stuff back in her bag and stuck it in the bedside cupboard along with her old copy of *Kidnapped* and a couple of newspaper reports I'd saved about the crash.

It wasn't much to show for a life.

I locked myself in the bathroom. That way, Doreen wouldn't hear the jerky sobs coming out of my throat. It was a long time before I came out again and opened the holdall. Inside it was a slim silver laptop, pretty new by the look of it. I booted it up, stared at the flashing *Enter Password* instruction, turned it off again and fished around

27

in the holdall. I pulled out a pen, some loose change, a soft black notebook and a glossy pamphlet about some big energy summit. I thumbed through it, looking at the photos of the speakers. It didn't matter if they were men, women, French, Chinese, Russian, American or British, they all had identical cheesy smiles and looked like they'd been stuffed. I flipped open the notebook. Except for a few scattered dates and a list of mobile numbers, it was just a jumble of squiggles like some kind of shorthand. Ramming my fingers into the pocket of the holdall, I dug out an envelope. I read the name on it. Once. Twice. Three times. Ivo Lincoln. It didn't mean the cops weren't jerks. It just made the mix-up a bit less random. I reached in the bedside cupboard for the newspaper cuttings, looking for the bit I'd read about Lincoln's dad. There it was: Professor Ralph Lincoln of St Saviour's College, Cambridge.

I went downstairs and asked to use the phone. Doreen got a bit shirty at first but gave in when I told her who I was calling. Directory enquiries put me through to something called the porters' lodge. This grumpy bloke said the Professor had taken time off for personal reasons. I said I'd call back. It wasn't just that Doreen's ears were flapping. There are some things you just can't leave in a message.

Doreen was doing the catering for some retirement do that night. George was very quiet while he heated up the lasagne she'd left us and he didn't say much till we'd almost finished eating it. Then he said, 'Is there anything you want to tell me?'

I shook my head. He got out his wallet. I shut my eyes.

This was it. He was about to kick me out. I was going to end up in care. I felt something being pushed into my hand. I opened my eyes. It was a twenty-pound note. George looked at me all sad and red-faced.

'You only had to ask, you know.'

He got up and started clearing the table.

'George . . .' I felt so guilty I just wanted to tell him everything. But I couldn't.

He wouldn't look at me.

'I'm sorry. It was for . . . a mate. He had an emergency.' My voice had gone wobbly with fear. 'Are you going to tell Doreen?'

He shook his head and headed for the kitchen. 'We both know what would happen if I did.'

CHAPTER 4

The tramp wasn't waiting in the dining room that night. I found him lying sweating in the cellar with his knife in one hand, my mobile in the other and Oz curled up next to him sound asleep. A single candle flickered in the corner, burning low. The tramp was gasping and flinching, murmuring something over and over that sounded like *tee gneeda paganaya*'.

I reached out to stroke Oz. The tramp's eyes sprang open and he made a feeble lunge at me with the knife. *'Ya zamochoo tebya!'*

Who knows what he was on about but he wasn't happy and he wasn't speaking French or German, I knew that much.

'It's OK. It's me, Joe. Remember? I've brought you medicine.'

He took a minute or two to calm down.

'Antibiotics and painkillers.' I said.

I sat him up and made him swallow a couple of tablets. He didn't want any of the lasagne I'd brought him and he slumped back, shivering and banging his teeth together while I made a fuss of Oz. I tried to tempt him with some dog biscuits. Weirdly, he wasn't that hungry. Maybe he'd been at the salami when the tramp was asleep.

'How this work?'

I turned round. The tramp was clutching my mobile, making trembly stabs at the buttons.

'Where've you been for the last decade?' I said, trying to be friendly.

He gave me a bleary look. 'In hell.'

Maybe I shouldn't have asked. He'd got a number scribbled on a scrap of newspaper. I punched it in and showed him how to make a call. When I told him we'd have to go upstairs to get a signal he groaned and said, 'Later, Joe. I go later.'

'You got a name?' I said.

He frowned for a minute as if he wasn't sure, then he said, 'Yuri'.

The sound of it seemed to upset him. He grabbed my hand. 'You no tell. They find me, they kill me.'

I wanted to believe he was crazy or lying, but the fear coming off him was like something you could touch.

'OK. I swear.'

'You get me new clothes, Joe?' He wasn't threatening or ordering now, just asking. 'I go to London.'

'All right,' I said, though the shape he was in, I couldn't

see him making it as far as the back gate.

He huddled down on the mattress, sweat dripping off his face.

'I'm taking Oz,' I said, getting ready to run if he tried to stop me.

'You come back tomorrow?' he murmured.

I stared at him, lying there, half dead with only me to help him, and heard myself say, 'Yeah'.

He let out a wheezy grunt. 'Do not come in day. Maybe someone see you.'

'OK.'

I stuck around till he fell asleep but left when his nightmares started. I had enough of my own to deal with.

If Yuri hadn't told me to stay clear of the house in daylight I'd have gone back next morning to see if he was OK. He was right, though. I couldn't chance some nosy dog walker spotting me going through the back gate and calling the cops, so I took Oz for a walk on the other side of the woods. He raced off, and I let him go. The trees along the path were tall and thick. One of them had keeled over with its roots in the air and its insides rotted out. It looked like I felt — empty and useless. I slumped against it, picking off the soggy bark and thinking about that creep Eddy Fletcher going round badmouthing Mum, accusing her of seeing Ivo Lincoln on the sly. Not that I'd have blamed her if she had. The stupid thing was, she'd never have cheated on Eddy because for some totally screwed-up reason that no one in their right mind could work out, she was crazy about him. But even I could see that her being in Lincoln's car that night was a bit weird.

A rumble like a muffled bass beat shook the ground. I swung round looking for Oz. Just as I heard a faint barking I spotted a horse and rider way off through the trees. I crashed towards the noise, speeding up as the yaps turned into squealy yelps. The rest of the soundtrack said it all. A screeching whinny, angry shouts and a sickening thud. I burst through the bushes. The horse was standing in a little clearing, all snorting and agitated, while Oz rushed around with his hackles high, barking at a boy on his backside in the dirt who was yelling: 'Shut up, you stupid dog!'

'He's not stupid, he's frightened. Oz, stop it. Come here!'

The boy turned round, his riding hat tipped sideways over his straggly blond fringe and his long freckly nose quivering like he'd just got a whiff of something rank.

'You're right. It's you who's stupid. If you can't control your dog, keep him on a lead.'

Talk about up himself. He looked about fifteen but he sounded like Prince Charles.

'Yeah, well he's more used to cars than horses,' I said, sticking out a hand to help him up.

Ignoring it, he struggled to his feet. 'So why don't you both go back where you came from and leave civilised people alone?'

He stomped after his horse, brushing the dirt off his trousers and muttering, 'Chav'.

'Prat!'

He gave me the finger without even bothering to turn round.

'C'mon, Oz.'

I trudged off, wondering how Mum had dealt with stuck-up losers like Horse-Boy when she'd lived round here, and imagining all the snappy put-downs I should have come up with to wipe that sneer off his beaky face. Course, if my mate Bailey had been around we'd have had a laugh about it, taken the mick out of his voice, turned it into a running gag. Made it all right. But Bailey wasn't around, and as far as I could see nothing was ever going to be all right again.

As soon as I got back to Laurel Cottage I went through the bags of clothes Doreen had left in the shed for the jumble. I picked out a pair of golf slacks, a couple of shirts and a green V-necked sweater of George's. The combination wasn't going to win Yuri any style awards but it was a lot less eye-catching than the filthy-blood-stained-rag look he was going for at the moment. Back in my room I threw in a bar of soap, a nail brush and my phone charger. It was only when I was searching for a decent pair of socks to give him that I realised Doreen had been snooping through my stuff. Not tidying it, just moving it very slightly.

Dinner that night was a kind of soggy rice pudding full of funny-looking mushrooms that smelled like they'd gone off. George raved about it, saying risotto was his favourite and no one could make it like his Dilly. But I bet you anything it was the remains of another catering job because I couldn't see our Doreen being fagged to make anything 'specially for him. After the business with the wallet I'd been worried she'd notice he was upset with me, but he was trying to hide it by making a big effort to keep the conversation going. I helped him out by asking for a list of chores I could do round the house. He said he'd have a think and smiled at me for the first time since he'd found out I was a thief. But Doreen wasn't smiling, no sirree, and there was an awkward silence before George flicked her a look and said, 'Your aunt and I heard from the education authority today.'

'Yeah?' I said.

'They've found you a place at a local school – Park Hill High. Unfortunately they can't take you until after the Easter holidays.'

That was nearly six weeks away. Doreen downed her wine in one gulp like she was fortifying herself for the task of getting shot of me well before then. After that the conversation kind of ground to a halt. But George didn't give up.

'I haven't seen your dog around,' he said. 'Is he OK?'

I was ready for this. 'He wandered off when we were in the woods but he came back as soon as he got hungry.'

He topped up Doreen's glass. 'Did you stumble across Saxted's notorious crime scene when you were down there?'

I looked up, not sure what he meant.

'In the woods. The boarded-up gates.'

My pulse was racketing. 'Oh . . . er, yeah. W-what is that place?'

'There used to be a lovely old house in there. What was it called, Dilly?' She shrugged. 'Saxted Grange, wasn't it? Yes, that's right, it had been in the Clairmont family for generations but it burned down in the sixties and Lord Greville Clairmont built a modern mansion on the site. I think his wife had a hand in the design – she was a famous model turned film actress – well, famous back then. Her name was Norma Craig.'

My mouth went dry. I glugged down some water, trying to act like the name meant nothing to me. But that must be her – Norma Craig, the slanty-eyed woman in all those photos. She'd even signed her initials – N.C. – on the picture I'd found on the floor.

George was on a roll now he'd finally found something to talk about, which was good because I wanted to know more.

'They called the new house Elysium,' he was saying. 'That means Paradise in Greek, or maybe it's Latin. Either way, it's ironic when you think what happened there.'

'Why? What did happen?'

George chewed his risotto and pointed his fork at Doreen.

'Dilly's the one to ask. Her mother used to work there.'

I shot a gobsmacked look at Doreen. 'Nan used to clean that house?'

'Don't use that vulgar expression. She wasn't your *nan*, she was your grandmother. And she was most certainly *not* a cleaner.'

'What was she then?'

'If you must know, she was a cocktail waitress.'

36

George laughed. 'According to your granddad, Pam Slattery mixed the meanest martini in the whole of Kent.'

That so didn't fit the warm fuzzy picture I'd always had of Mum's mum baking, knitting and generally doing other nan-type activities.

'The Clairmonts threw so many parties they had half the village in to help,' George went on.

'So go on, what happened up there?'

George leant across the table. 'A murder.'

A shiver skidded down my back.

'Who did it?'

'Lord Clairmont.'

'Who'd he kill?'

'The papers said he intended to kill Norma Craig, but the house was dark and he murdered the housekeeper by mistake. The story was splashed all over the headlines for weeks.'

'What happened to Clairmont?'

'He vanished. Most people think his millionaire friends spirited him out of the country before the police had even found his car abandoned on the coast.'

'What about Norma Craig?'

'She had some kind of breakdown, went off to a clinic in Switzerland and never came back.'

I looked at Doreen. 'Did the police interview my na . . . your mum about the murder?'

'Why would they? My parents moved to Yorkshire months before it happened.'

That was news to me. 'I thought they'd always lived in Saxted.'

'You thought wrong.'

The lines round her mouth were getting deeper but I kept going. 'So why did they leave?'

'My father got a transfer up north for a while and stuck me in a school where I was bullied rotten.' She paused but only to draw breath. 'He told me to put a brave face on it so as not to upset my mother. Then, after Sadie came along they moved back and practically forgot I existed.'

Get over it, Doreen. At least you had parents. And a home.

'Is Clairmont still alive?' I said.

When Doreen didn't answer, George said, 'No one knows, but even after all this time the courts still won't declare him dead.'

'Why not?'

'Because from the day he disappeared people have been claiming they've spotted him all over the world. Someone thought they sighted him last year in Goa. Some old beach bum got the shock of his life when the press turned up in helicopters and surrounded his hut. If you're interested in the case your grandmother saved all the cuttings. They'll probably be in that box of books I got down from the attic. Have a look.'

Doreen chipped in then, reminding him it was time for some gardening show they wanted to watch, which was my cue to get lost. That was fine by me. I went straight upstairs and upended the box of books, tossing aside the old paperbacks, mags and cookbooks until I found a bulging scrapbook. I undid the faded ribbon and looked inside. Mum always said that Nan was a hoarder and it looked like she was right. Nan had stuck in just about everything from her time at Elysium – articles about Norma Craig, menu cards, pictures of a buffet laid out round an ice sculpture shaped like a bear, guest lists, wine labels, invitations, signed photos of old-time celebs like Ringo Starr, Mick Jagger and Cilla Black and a load of others I'd never heard of. There was one shot of the staff lined up with Norma and Clairmont on the terrace. They all looked so glamorous that if Nan hadn't written their names and jobs round the edge you'd have thought they were guests. There was Jeff the chauffeur in a peaked cap and flash suit; Jean-Luc the chef, all dark hair and curly moustache; Nan with blonde, flicked-up hair and thick eye make-up; and Harry the gardener, who looked like he'd stepped straight out of Hollywood, right down to the chiselled features, muscly arms and torso-hugging T-shirt. It wasn't that surprising. According to one of the articles Nan had saved, ugly people never got a look in with Norma Craig. She'd even had this stupid catchphrase, 'only the beautiful'. What an airhead.

I kept turning the pages. Suddenly Nan's souvenirs stopped and the cuttings about the murder began. The papers had certainly got their money's worth but what got me was that it was all *Norma Craig this* and *Greville Clairmont that*. No one gave a monkey's about the woman he'd killed. It took me ages to even find her name. Janice Gribben. She was always just *the housekeeper*, like she was some stray dog that got run over in the street. And as for printing a decent photo of her, no chance. They'd all used the same side-on shot of her, caught in the background while Norma Craig was schmoozing some bigwig. Janice's face was so small and blurry they'd had to circle it in red in case you missed it. She hadn't been that old when she died, only twenty-nine – six years younger than Mum.

I felt my insides churning. The papers had treated Mum exactly the same way. *Occasional pub singer* Sadie Slattery hardly got a look in while the articles went on and on about *star journalist Ivo Lincoln killed in tragic hit and run*. They were even setting up a bursary for trainee journalists in his name. What was anyone doing in Mum's name? Half the papers hadn't even spelled it right.

CHAPTER 5

When Oz and I got to Elysium that night I was amazed to see Yuri looking a bit better and I felt like Santa when he started unpacking the clothes I'd brought him. I'd gone upstairs to boil some water to clean his leg, and I was standing in the hall getting creeped out by the thought of a murder happening there when I felt a hand on my shoulder. I nearly had a heart attack but it was only Yuri.

'I need bath, Joe,' he said.

He was right about that. He stank.

'Find a bathroom and get something you can use as a towel. I'll heat you some water.'

He pointed up to the landing. 'Two doors from stairs there is bathroom.'

'OK.' He'd obviously been getting to know his way around.

I dug out the biggest saucepans I could find, boiled some water and made a couple of trips lugging them upstairs. The bathroom didn't have any windows so I stood the torch on the floor, filling the space with rings of dim blue light. The walls looked like they were covered in white marble, there was a matching bath sunk into the floor and all the taps were gold and shaped like dolphins. Yuri came in and pulled off his grubby shirt. Suddenly I wished I'd left it dark. His back and arms were like something out of a horror comic. The bits that weren't seared with wrinkly red scars were tattooed all over with spiders, stars, snarling wolves and a building crowded with towers and turban-shaped domes. He turned around. I heard my breath catch. A one-eyed skull was leering at me through the twist of barbed wire circling his chest. Maybe he hadn't been joking when he said he'd been in hell.

I shut the door on him, took Oz for a midnight run in the garden and tried to blank out Yuri's tattoos by picturing the windows of Elysium blazing with light and Greville Clairmont, Norma Craig and their glitzy mates out on the terrace dancing, drinking my nan's cocktails, and diving into the pool. But all the time I kept thinking about the murder and seeing one-eyed skulls forming in the shadows. I went back to the cellar, lit a couple more candles and started laying out the food I'd brought. As I shoved Yuri's old coat to one side I felt something hard and heavy bump the side of the workbench. Glancing round, I dipped my hand in the pocket and pulled out the old Oxo tin I'd seen the first time I came. Holding my breath, I rubbed the dried mud off the hinges and pried back the lid.

Blimey, Yuri. Where'd you get this lot?

It was full of jewels. Poking my fingers through the glittering stash, I separated a diamond-studded tie-clip with matching cufflinks, and a necklace, earrings and bracelet all made of big green stones. If they were real emeralds they had to be worth a mint.

The thump of Yuri's feet in the hall jerked my jaw shut and my brain back into gear, but I only just got the tin back in his coat before he limped in, buttoning up one of his new shirts. I stopped feeling like Santa and started feeling more like Baron Frankenstein watching his monster rise from the slab. Scrubbed up, Yuri looked almost human and he smelled of Doreen's lavender soap. He sat on the mattress, letting Oz climb up next to him, while I put a new bandage on his leg. The wound was still disgusting, and the red had taken on a nasty greenish tinge.

'How did you do this?' I asked.

'They take me to forest to kill me. I fight with driver and car turn over. Everyone is hurt and I get away.'

'Who's *they?*'

He spat on the floor. 'Bad people.'

I could see he was getting angry so I changed the subject quick.

'Any luck with your phone call?' I said.

'I leave many messages. I tell him they try to kill me. He no call back.'

He'd switched from angry to upset. To cheer him up I handed him the mini cheesecake I'd nicked from one of Doreen's fridges. He shoved the whole thing in his mouth, chewed for a bit then frowned at me.

'Why you live with your aunt?'

I was amazed he'd remembered. 'My mum . . . she . . . died in a car crash.'

'When?'

'Couple of . . . weeks ago.'

I could feel my eyes welling up. I snatched up his smelly blanket, turned away and started shaking out the dog hairs so he wouldn't see me cry. The tears kept coming and I kept flapping that blanket like a crazy bullfighter.

Yuri's strong, bony hands caught my shoulders and swung me round to face him.

'When you think of her, it hurt bad. Yes?'

Shut up! Shut up! I don't wanna talk about it!

'This hurt is good,' he said.

Angry now, I pulled away, wiping my eyes. 'How d'you make that out?'

He thumped his chest with his fist. 'It keep her alive in your heart.'

I stared at him for the longest time, totally thrown by what he'd said. But I tell you one thing, it made a change from the usual garbage people come out with when you tell them your mum's just died.

It wasn't the crash dream that woke me next morning. It was George, coming in to say goodbye before he left for Germany. He'd been really decent about that money and I was sorry he was going.

'I want you to do your best to keep your aunt happy while I'm gone,' he said.

'I'll try.' I picked at the duvet cover. 'Did you think of any jobs for me to do? I really want to pay you back for . . . you know, what I took.'

'Don't worry about it, Joe. But if you really want to help me out there is one thing you could do. Do you like cars?'

'Kind of.'

I didn't tell him that round Farm Street, 'liking' cars meant nicking old bangers, taking them for a joy ride and setting fire to what was left.

'I bought an old Spitfire last year, fancied doing it up. But with things getting a bit tight money-wise Dilly wants me to get rid of it. So if you could give it a good clean I'll put it on the market when I get back.'

'No problem,' I said, really glad he'd come up with something I could do to help him out.

'It's in the garage.' He sighed and walked to the door. 'I'll be sad to see it go.'

'Hope you get the contract,' I said.

He turned and nodded, and for the first time I saw the strain behind his smile. 'Yes, Joe, so do I.'

Oz just didn't get it that the hose wasn't alive. He went into full attack mode every time the water sprayed his way. He made so much noise that Doreen came out to complain and caught me at the wheel trying to work out the controls with Oz riding shotgun beside me. She threatened to lock him in the shed if he didn't pipe down and pointed out a couple of dirty marks I'd missed on the bonnet.

Still, by the end of the day I'd got that little red two-seater hoovered, washed, waxed and polished to such a gleaming shine that even she couldn't find anything to moan about.

She was working that night so I had a cheese toastie in front of the telly. By the time I'd watched a couple of movies and read a bit more of *Kidnapped* I was beginning to feel a bit calmer. Yuri wasn't about to die on me, George looked like he'd forgiven me, and Doreen hadn't noticed the missing food.

Boy, had I underestimated Doreen.

Around midnight I was poking around in one of her freezers when she burst in covered in face cream, dressing gown flapping, screaming her head off. 'I knew you were a thieving little scumbag the minute you walked into this house and now I've caught you red-handed.'

I played innocent.

'Sorry, Aunt Doreen . . . I got hungry. I thought you wouldn't mind.'

The good news was that my backpack was still in the hall so she hadn't caught me stuffing it with food. The bad news was that I was holding a portion of frozen venison casserole in a foil tub, which isn't most kids' idea of a late-night snack. I'd been planning to heat it up when I got to Elysium and give Yuri a treat. *Go on, Joe. Explain that away.*

She grabbed it out of my hand. 'Venison!'

'Oh, sorry ... I thought it was . . . ice cream.'

Not bad, Joe, not bad at all. Now keep smiling and maintain eye contact. Whatever you do, don't look guilty.

'Go to your room, now!'

I hung around with my ear to my bedroom door, waiting for her to go back to bed like any normal person. She didn't, though. Not Doreen. From the smell of it she was brewing up a gallon of industrial-strength coffee, and when I peeked over the bannister, she was sat in the lounge with a thermos and the door wide open, staking out the stairs. I retreated to my room and gave it an hour or so before I sneaked down, hoping she'd dropped off to sleep. But she was just sitting there and had a fit when she saw me. I mumbled something about a drink of water and beat it back upstairs. Yuri would have to go hungry for one night. I just hoped he wouldn't think I'd abandoned him.

In the morning, Doreen was still prowling around like a Doberman in a goods yard, so I got out of there double-quick and used some of the twenty-pound note George had given me to get Yuri two sausage rolls and a Mars Bar from the village shop.

Soon as I hit the woods I saw fresh tyre marks on the track. I started to run, panicked that it was cops arresting Yuri or hit men come to finish what they'd started. As I got nearer I saw that the metal panels that had been covering the gateway had been torn down, revealing a carved, stone archway and a pair of iron gates that were standing wide open. There were vans on the drive. Things went misty. I kept running, though my legs were like rubber and my breath wouldn't come.

The mist cleared. It wasn't cops or hit men. It was an army of workmen, swarming round the house, lugging ladders up the steps, clambering on to the roof and clearing the garden. I dodged behind a tree and watched a big blonde woman hauling some weird contraption bristling with nozzles out of a van that said Queens of Kleen down the side. A stressed-looking bloke came over and started shoving his clipboard under her nose and giving her a right mouthful. She wasn't having it. She shouted back that all her people had been working flat out since the crack of dawn and if he wanted things done any faster he could give Mary bleedin' Poppins a call. He stormed off and started having a go at the painters.

I lobbed a stick over the wall and hissed at Oz, 'Go on, boy. Fetch!'

Not being a stick-fetching sort of dog he watched it go and went back to biting his bum. So I waved the sausage roll around and chucked that. That got him going and once he was through the gate I ran in, yelling at him to come back. He threw me a look like I should make up my bloody mind, wolfed the sausage roll and peed up the wheel of the Queens of Kleen van. I rushed over to the blonde woman, saying I was sorry about my dog and how he wasn't used to the gates being open. She didn't care and she didn't want to chat. I went on pushing.

'Was there . . . er . . . anybody living here, you know, squatters or anything?'

'A few mice and spiders.'

'I couldn't take a look around inside, could I?'

She frowned. 'Why?'

'My nan, she used to work here years ago . . . she's not well. It'd really perk her up if I could tell her what it looks like now.'

'Oh, go on then – five minutes.'

Oz cut ahead of me and made straight for the cellar. The door was open. I raced down after him. He skittered to a stop and let out a whiny bark.

Yuri had gone. All that was left was his bedding, his old clothes and a couple of burnt-out candle stumps. I should have been punching air that he'd managed to get away. Instead I crouched on the bottom step feeling as if someone had torn out my insides and tossed them in the trash. Who cared if Yuri was a crook or a loony or even a murderer? Looking after him had filled a great big hole in my life, and now he was gone.

I reached for his torn trousers, feeling through the pockets in the crazy hope he'd left me a note. All I found was the crumpled scrap of newspaper scrawled with the number he'd been so desperate to ring.

Oz sat looking at me, tail sweeping the floor, like he expected me to bring Yuri back.

I threw down the trousers. 'Sorry, Oz. That's it. He's gone.'

People were stomping into the room above, slamming doors, dragging furniture around, and I could hear Clipboard Man yelling at everyone to get a move on. I wiped my nose across my sleeve and trudged upstairs.

Light was pouring in through the newly cleaned windows and the whole house was filling with the sounds of hoovering, banging and voices. It was strange. I felt this sudden kick of sadness that I wouldn't be coming back.

A younger, bored-looking Queen of Kleen with dyed black hair was having a fag by the van.

'Who's moving in?' I asked.

She took a long drag and blew out the smoke. 'Some old biddy called Norma Craig.'

As I ran through the woods, I glanced back at the house. For the first time I noticed the carving on the arch above the gates. It was two prancing bears holding up a shield, identical to the crest on the key ring Yuri had given me. I didn't fancy getting caught with a set of keys that easy to identify so I pushed them deep between the roots of the big oak tree by the side door and kicked a pile of leaves over the top.

The news about Norma Craig was sweeping through the village like a flash flood. On my way back, I passed a huddle of dog walkers gossiping about the murder, got stopped by a couple of people asking the way to Elysium and saw a TV van with a big satellite dish on the roof heading down the track. It looked like Norma Craig was still big news. All I cared about was Yuri. I wanted to believe he'd be fine. After all, he'd got George's money, clean clothes, and all those jewels. Not to mention my phone. My phone! I was an idiot. I could call him and see if he was OK.

Doreen was out when I got back to Laurel Cottage so I used the phone in the kitchen, leaning against the work-top to dial the number. It went straight to voicemail. Damn. The battery was probably flat. I jiggled the receiver, watched Oz digging up Doreen's roses and tried to think what else I could do. Suddenly I was searching my jeans, rooting through all the pockets. After a burst of panic, I felt my fingers curl round the scrap of newspaper Yuri had left in the cellar. I let out a whoop of relief. Maybe he'd finally got through to the bloke he'd been trying to phone. Maybe he was with him now. I jabbed in the number.

It rang once before a man's voice came on the line – young, posh, sure of himself.

'*You've reached the voicemail of Ivo Lincoln. Sorry I can't take your call. Leave a message and I'll get back to you as soon as I can.*'

I dropped the receiver and threw up in Doreen's shiny sink.

CHAPTER 6

Doreen had one of those waste-disposal units that grinds up trash and slurps it away, so dealing with the puke was easy. Sorting the mess in my head was going to take a bit longer. One minute Lincoln was giving Mum a lift in London, the next Yuri was calling him from Saxted. Who was this guy? I'd never even heard of him till a couple of weeks ago and now his fingerprints were smeared all over my life. And every time his name cropped up things turned nasty.

Still feeling sick, I called St Saviour's College. This time the guy in the porters' lodge said the Professor was around, so I left my number and a message to call me urgently. Then I fetched down Lincoln's holdall from my room, and laid out all his stuff on the worktop. I switched on the laptop and looked at the password box. The answer

– or at least some it – had to be here. I wandered round the kitchen – opening drawers, staring out the window, twanging the knives in the knife rack – trying to piece together everything I knew about Ivo Lincoln.

According to the papers, he'd been a real wonder boy and, if the pictures were anything to go by, quite good-looking – for a lanky, long-haired toff. Which was why Eddy had got so steamed up about Mum being in his car. Most of the reports said she'd cadged a lift off him because it was raining and she'd had a few too many. I'd gone along with that, just to shut Eddy up, but deep down it had always grated. First, Mum had sworn to me that she'd cut her drinking down to one glass of wine a night. Second she had a rule about never getting lifts from strangers after gigs. She was so paranoid about it she'd done a deal with an all-female minicab service who always drove her home. So even if it *was* tipping it down that night and posh boy Lincoln *wasn't* coming across as a perv or an axe murderer, why chance it? But then, if she wasn't cadging a lift and she wasn't cheating on Eddy, what had she been doing with Lincoln? And something else was bugging me. How come Yuri had decided to hole up in the exact same village that Mum had grown up and been buried in?

I'd gone round in a circle, got nowhere and ended up right back where I'd started. But Lincoln being a journalist kept throwing up another possibility; one I was having real trouble getting my head round. Was there a chance that Mum had been helping him with a story? It didn't seem likely. Not unless he'd been doing a feature on thirty-something singers who still had dreams of hitting the big time. Yuri on the other hand . . . well, he coincided a lot more closely with my idea of someone a hot-shot reporter might want to talk to – on the run, up to his tattooed neck in all sorts of dodgy stuff, and petrified that 'bad people' were trying to kill him. Come to think of it, could that be why they were trying to kill him, to stop him selling information to Lincoln?

A terrible thought began circling the edges of my brain. I made a supreme effort to shut it out but it waltzed in anyway, making my breath stop and the room start pitching around. The hospital had given me a leaflet that said grief did funny things to your brain and you shouldn't be surprised if you started 'indulging in fantasy as an outlet for your emotions'. I'd chucked it straight in the bin but now I did a quick bit of DIY counselling and told myself to get real before I cracked up. It didn't work and even sticking my head under the cold tap couldn't slosh away the horrible feeling that I was on to something. The phone rang. I lurched across the room and grabbed it.

'Hello?'

'Is that Joe Slattery?'

'Yeah.'

'Ralph Lincoln.'

Weirdly, he pronounced it *Rafe*, like it rhymed with 'safe'.

'Oh, right . . . um, thanks for calling back. I'm . . . Sadie Slattery's son. I don't know if you remember me. We met . . . at the hospital.'

'Of course I remember you, Joe. How are you bearing

54

up?' He sounded old and tired.

'Um . . . OK.'

'Still in London?'

'No, Kent. With Mum's sister.'

'How's that working out?'

'Oh, you know. She and Mum weren't exactly close.'

'That must very difficult for all of you. So how can I help you, Joe?'

'There's been a mix-up with Mum and Ivo's stuff.'

'I don't follow.'

'The bags in the car. The police sent me Ivo's as well as Mum's.'

He made a faint sound, somewhere between a sob and a groan.

'It's got his laptop and a notebook in it and . . . '

'I'll . . . organise a courier to pick them up.'

'OK, but . . . um . . . before I get his laptop back to you I was wondering if you'd mind me taking a look through his files.'

'Whatever for?'

I took a breath. 'Have you ever wondered if there might be a link between the crash and a story he was investigating?'

He went so quiet I thought the phone had gone dead.

'Professor, are you there?'

'Yes, I'm here.'

'Have you . . . ever wondered that?'

'Listen to me, Joe. When someone young and healthy dies an untimely death, those left behind automatically search for answers to take away the senselessness of their

55

loss. It's a natural part of the grieving process.' The hospital had obviously given him the same leaflet. 'So yes, I did consider the possibility that Ivo's death had not been accidental. In the end, however, I had to accept that what happened to my son was just a hideous and arbitrary case of hit and run.'

'Well, sir' – the 'sir' slipped out like I was talking to a teacher – 'I'm still at the looking-for-answers stage, so would you mind if I asked you a couple of questions?'

He sighed. 'Very well.'

'What *was* Ivo working on?'

'I'm sorry to disappoint you, Joe. A prolonged assignment in Afghanistan had left him so exhausted he'd taken a break. Ironic, isn't it, that he survived the dangers of Helmand only to die on the streets of North London?'

'How long was he off work?'

'A month. I wanted him to take longer but there's a big energy summit coming up and he'd been asked to profile some of the delegates.'

'Did he go away anywhere?'

'Yes. Kiev.'

'Where's that?'

'Ukraine. It's the capital. He'd studied there for a while, got to know it pretty well.'

'Ukraine . . . that's in . . . Eastern Europe?' I said, wishing I'd kicked the habit of nodding off in Geography.

'Yes. Part of the former Soviet Union.'

'So they speak what . . . Russian?'

'For the most part. Some local dialects as well, I believe.'

Was that Russian Yuri had been muttering in his sleep? Had Ivo met him in *Ukraine?* My heart punched my ribs so loudly I was sure the Prof could hear it down the phone. I needn't have worried. He was too busy warbling on about Ivo getting a first class degree in Slavonic studies – whatever they were.

I knew nothing about Ukraine except for this documentary me and Mum had watched about a macho undercover reporter on the trail of a huge money laundering operation. He'd ended up in Kiev and got beaten up by a gang of sleazy thugs who'd discovered his secret camera and didn't fancy being on telly.

'Aren't journalists always on the lookout for stories, even when they're on holiday?' I asked. 'Aren't there masses of gangs over there?' Cogs whirred in my brain. *Gangs run by the kind of 'bad people' who were after Yuri.*

'Joe, I know you're confused and unhappy, but think about it logically. If Ukrainian mobsters wanted to get rid of Ivo, why wait until he got back to England? And why pick a method as risky and uncertain as running his car off the road? It makes no sense.'

'It would if they wanted to get rid of Ivo *and* Mum.'

The words hung there, raw and shocking. I couldn't believe I'd actually thought them, let alone said them out loud.

'You're not telling me your mother had links with the Ukrainian Mafia, are you?'

'Not that she was letting on.'

He made a grunty noise, like he almost laughed, and his voice relaxed a bit.

'As far as I know, Ivo wasn't working on anything at all in Ukraine. So you see: no sinister investigations on the go, no forays into the criminal underworld.'

I wasn't buying that but I'd sworn to Yuri I wouldn't betray him so I trod carefully,

'I . . . er . . . still wouldn't mind having a look in his laptop.'

I heard a sigh and then a scratchy sound like he was rubbing his chin. 'Oh, very well. If it will set your mind at rest.'

Yes! I jabbed the air but tried to keep my voice calm. 'Do you know his password?'

'I think he used Bitsy241 for pretty much everything. It was a family joke, you see. Bitsy's his twin, two for one.'

Why did posh people have such weird names?

I pulled Ivo's laptop towards me. It was top of the range, even had built in mobile broadband. I typed in Bitsy241, pressed Enter and felt a nervous buzz as his desktop flashed on to the screen. 'Brilliant. Thanks.' My fingers brushed the keyboard, itching to get into his files.

'When did he go to Ukraine?'

'The beginning of February.'

'When did he get back?'

'The day before the crash, which meant I hadn't seen him for over a month before he died. And that was just for a quick coffee on a fleeting visit to town. You never think, do you, that it might be the last time?'

A stab of pain snatched my breath. The last I'd seen of Mum was the edge of her coat whisking through the door as she'd rushed off to the Trafalgar Arms. On her way out she'd kissed the top of my head and told me not to stay up too late, but I'd been so engrossed in *Doctor Who* I hadn't looked up. *Don't go there, Joe.* I leant my head against the wall and swallowed hard.

'So this courier . . . when are you sending him?' I said.

'Whenever suits . . . unless . . . well, if you had time to bring Ivo's things to Cambridge I'd be delighted to give you lunch in college. I'd pay your travel costs, of course.' His voice was getting gruffer and I knew what was coming. 'It might help you to talk to someone who understands what you're going through.'

No, it wouldn't. No way. But if I went to Cambridge I could go on picking his brain about Ivo.

'OK. Yeah. Thanks. How about tomorrow?'

'Unfortunately I'm teaching all day. How are you fixed for the day after?'

My breathing got calmer as we discussed normal stuff like train times. But my brain was still playing up – flooding one minute, stalling the next.

'Excellent, that's settled then. But Joe …'

'Yeah?'

'The sooner you forget these crazy notions, the sooner you'll begin to move on.'

He rang off. I tapped into Ivo Lincoln's files.

What? That couldn't be right.

Lincoln had only got six saved documents. I wiped my sweaty palms on my jeans and opened the first one. It was an insurance claim form, downloaded on 4 March, the morning of the crash, for stuff he'd had stolen the day before. I scrolled through it.

Name: Ivo Horatio (you're kidding me) Lincoln
Place of theft: Oselya Guest House, Strizhavka, Ukraine
Items stolen: Apple Mac laptop, Samsung camera, leather bag, books

I was gutted. Everything he'd written in Ukraine would be on the stolen laptop. He must have bought this one as soon as he got back. The other documents were all letters to banks, building societies and credit card companies, trying to sort out his money. Not a whiff of any heavy-duty investigations. Not a mention of Mum or Yuri.

I tried the Bitsy password on his emails, felt my heart speed up when it worked and started scrolling through his messages. Now I know you shouldn't speak ill of the dead but Jes-us this guy was boring – and so were his mates. No jokes, no funny YouTube clips, just dreary press releases about nuclear energy and the 'struggle for justice' in places I couldn't pronounce.

Maybe I was crazy. Maybe Mum getting killed in Ivo Lincoln's car and Yuri having Lincoln's number was just one of those wacky coincidences you read about on the internet, you know – random man answers public phone on crowded station and it's his long-lost brother calling. For all I knew, Yuri could turn out to be Polish, Hungarian or Swedish, which would blast the Ukrainian connection to rubble. I picked up the scrap of newspaper with Ivo's phone number on it. There was a tiny line of print above the scribble. I squinted hard, trying to make it out.

Факты и комментарии.

Letter by letter, I checked the words against a site listing foreign alphabets. It was Russian all right. Spelled out in English it said *Fakty i Kommentarii* – which, according to Wikipedia, was the biggest-selling tabloid in Ukraine. I was right. Yuri was Ukrainian! It might not sound like much of a breakthrough but I felt like I'd bought a winning scratch card.

Tyres crunched on the drive. Doreen was home. I logged off, scooped up Lincoln's stuff and bolted to my room. Halfway there I realised I'd left his notebook behind and I was heading back to get it when the phone rang. I heard Doreen come in the back door and pick up in the kitchen. I'd thought it might be the Professor calling back but it was obviously someone for Doreen. She was putting on her poshest voice and letting out chirps of fake laughter between comments like, 'Yes, indeed, Mr Pritchard . . .', 'What an honour . . .', 'Such a remarkable woman . . .'

I hung back, watching her through the bannister, waiting for her to finish. She was smiling and patting her hairdo, though as usual there wasn't one single hair out of place.

'Oh, of course. In my line of work, discretion is everything. I like to think my regular clients regard me as a trusted personal friend.' Suddenly the smile froze. 'I don't understand. That really wouldn't be . . .'

The caller interrupted and she changed her tune pretty quick.

'No. No, Mr Pritchard, that won't be necessary. I always try to accommodate my client's wishes, however unorthodox

they may be. If you send me a list of her dietary require-
ments, I'll prepare some menus. But there may be a
problem with that arrangement longer term, you see . . .'

I missed the next bit because, for once, she lowered her
voice and I had to edge a bit nearer to hear more. '. . . in
fact, given my nephew's situation I wonder if I might ask
you for a little professional advice . . .'

Hang on. Why was she talking about me?

I leant even closer and got my answer.

'. . . it's only natural that the boy should want to be
with his father now he's lost his mother and I . . . that
is . . . my husband and I were wondering how best to go
about finding him.'

Well, good luck with that, Doreen. Mum had been trying to
track down my dad for fourteen years but Adam Okampo
was slicker than the Invisible Man when it came to disap-
pearing. Still, I s'pose I couldn't blame Doreen for giving
it a go. And getting dumped with a dad who'd never
wanted me couldn't be any worse than living with an
aunt who thought I was scum.

Doreen went on listening for a couple of minutes but
there was no laughter, fake or otherwise, when she said
goodbye. From the way she rammed the handset down it
seemed like this Pritchard guy had rubbed her right up
the wrong way.

CHAPTER 7

For dinner that night Doreen heated up a couple of portions of her latest creation, fish tagine with minted couscous — don't ask — and we'd been sitting at opposite ends of the table silently pushing it round our plates for at least five minutes when she sniffed and said, 'Norma Craig's lawyer contacted me earlier.'

My skin went prickly. So that's who she'd been talking to.

'Miss Craig has heard about my reputation for high-quality cuisine and total discretion, and she's decided that once she moves back to Elysium she wants me to supply her with an evening meal two or three times a week.'

'That's great,' I said, though Doreen didn't seem too thrilled about it. In fact, from the way she was screwing up her lips you'd have thought she'd just spotted a dead rat in her couscous.

'Of course, I couldn't say no but I'm far too busy to do the deliveries myself. I told him . . . *you'd* have to do them.'

'Me?'

'Why not?'

'Oh, no reason. It's just that . . . you know, with some-one famous like Norma Craig I thought you'd want to do the face-to-face yourself.'

Now what had I said? She was fuming.

'I can't just abandon my regular clients because some washed-up old celebrity wants my services. Who does she think she is anyway? She might have married a lord but everyone knows her father was a crook. If he hadn't dropped dead of a heart attack he'd have ended up in jail with the rest of his gangster cronies.'

Calm down, Doreen. What's Norma Craig ever done to you?

'OK,' I said. 'No probs. I'll do the deliveries.'

'That dog of yours has been digging up my roses.'

'Sorry.'

I forced down a couple more mouthfuls and scarpered upstairs, trying to work out what was going on. Doreen snapping at me was nothing unusual but after all that *'What an honour, she's a remarkable woman'* stuff she'd been giving Pritchard on the phone, the sudden downer on Norma Craig was more than weird. Still, I'd got bigger things to worry about.

I pulled Lincoln's laptop on to my knees and went back to his emails, checking for messages to or from news-papers, sent around the time he was in Ukraine. I waded through loads from girls with names like Chloe, Emma, Zara and Abbie, all badgering him with invites to dinners and parties. I don't know why they bothered; half the time he never even replied.

I kept going and nearly missed a message he'd sent to a man called Stephen Dawes at *The Times*. It was dated 12 Feb – three weeks before the crash.

> Stephen,
>
> *What would you say to a piece on Kiev's latest tourist attraction – the recently opened KGB Archive? I'd like to follow up some of the human dramas documented in the files, interview survivors and/or their families and compare their take on events with the official government version. I could do a bit of groundwork while I'm here and come back after the energy summit.*
>
> Ivo

The *KGB archive?* That didn't sound like much of a tourist attraction. Though I s'pose Mum might have been tempted. She'd always loved spy thrillers, 'specially those old black and white ones with blokes in hats and trench coats lurking under lamp posts. Personally I prefer movies with a bit less hanging around and a bit more action. But even Mum might have been put off by the photo Ivo had attached of the grim-looking KGB headquarters, not to mention the caption that came with it:

> 'The secret service of the Soviet Union, the KGB, was responsible for terrible crimes against humanity. The Soviet Union is no more; and the KGB sank into oblivion with it. But it has left behind an

enormous amount of archive material which the government of
Ukraine has now made accessible to the general public.'

But it looked like this Stephen Dawes had been up for
an article.

Sounds good. See what you come up with and we'll talk when
you're back in UK.

S

My heart speeded up. So Ivo *had* been working on a
story in Ukraine, or at least thinking about it. A search for
Stephen Dawes turned up about twenty more messages
but they were all at least three months old and didn't even
mention Ukraine.

I Googled *KGB archive Kiev* and got a news clip of a
reporter walking down a long row of neatly numbered
cardboard boxes, pulling out yellowing files and chatting
away to a smiley, clean-cut curator who'd got his answers
all prepared.

'Opening the archive is part of the healing process,' he
said in bumpy English. 'It is a way of coming to terms
with difficult aspects of our country's Soviet past.'

'I understand there's been some resistance to a
complete declassification of the material,' the reporter
said.

'Yes, and I admit we have had to be somewhat selective
about declassifying more recent files, given that some of
the agents involved may still be alive. However, I am

confident that, with time, all such obstacles will be removed.'

Yeah, right. Whatever the government was saying about openness it didn't look like they'd be leaving any real secrets lying around for just anyone to look at. Even so, when the final shot froze on a close-up of one of the boxes, identical to the millions of others stacked on the shelves, I got a burning urge to know which ones Ivo Lincoln had opened and exactly what he'd found inside.

Given the atmosphere at Laurel Cottage I reckoned it would suit Doreen best if I skipped breakfast and kept well out of her way till dinner time. So you can guess what a surprise I got when I was slinking past the kitchen next morning and she called out a sharp, 'Come here!'

I doubled back, slowly.

'You've got post,' she said.

She put down her coffee cup and slid two letters across the table, using the tip of her red-painted nail, like the envelopes might be infected or something. But I could tell she was dying to know what was in them.

'Cheers,' I said, picking up a white one with the St Saviour's crest on the front. 'This'll be a train ticket from Professor Lincoln.' She looked impressed. 'He's invited me to lunch.'

It was the thick brown envelope, addressed in funny spidery writing — *Jo Slatery, Lorel Cotage, Saxted, Kent* — that was bothering me.

She was watching me, tapping the table with her nail.

'. . . and this one'll be . . . from my mate Bailey.'

She wasn't to know that Bailey was about as likely to send me snail mail as he was to take up belly dancing. I sauntered slowly across the lawn to the shed, feeling Doreen's eyes burning into my scalp, and waited till I'd slammed the door and taken a couple of deep breaths before ripping open the envelope. A twist of grubby paper fell out and something sparkly clattered to the floor. Oz gave it a sniff. It was a narrow gold bar with a fastening on the back like a badge. I picked it up. My old headmaster used to wear something a bit like it clipped to his tie, only his wasn't gold and it didn't have a stonking great diamond in the middle of it held up by a couple of prancing bears. My hands went clammy. That was the crest on the keys to Elysium, and on the archway over the gate. There was no message with it but I knew exactly who'd sent me this tie-clip. It was Yuri. And how did I know that? Because I'd seen it before. In that old Oxo tin he'd had in the cellar of Elysium. And just like the other jewels in there, this looked pretty real to me. This was his way of saying thanks and letting me know he was all right, I couldn't chance Doreen finding it and asking difficult questions so I carefully clipped it to the top of my boxers. The diamond dug into my stomach every time I moved, but at least I'd always know where it was.

Oz was jumping up, ready to get going, but I went on squinting at the postmark on the envelope, trying to make out where Yuri had posted it. It looked like London somewhere but the rest was too smudged to read. I folded it up, stuffed it in my pocket and fed Oz. Then I took him for a long walk, right through the village and round to the river. When I got back I nicked a bit of paper out of next door's recycling, scribbled a spidery note asking me how things were going, signed it 'from Bailey' and left it by my bed, all ready for Doreen to find next time she fancied a snoop through my stuff.

CHAPTER 8

I spent the journey to Cambridge flicking through Ivo Lincoln's notebook, trying to stop Oz climbing on the seats and worrying about Yuri. There was a chance that he'd flogged the rest of that jewellery and gone off to sun himself in the Caribbean, but deep down I was scared he was sick again, lying all alone in some abandoned building muttering to himself like a crazy man. Wherever he was I had to track him down. He was my only chance of finding out why Mum had been in Lincoln's car.

The train whooshed into darkness, filling my ears with a juddery roar. Should I tell Professor Lincoln about Yuri? The answer jolted from yes to no with every sway of the carriage. As soon as I got off and saw him standing at the ticket barrier in his woolly scarf and posh tweed suit I knew I couldn't risk it. He was definitely the kind of bloke who thought coming clean to the police was the answer to everything. His swept-back hair was thinner and greyer than I'd remembered, his lanky body seemed more stooped and even though he was making a big effort to look cheerful his face was rigid, like a sad face mask. Maybe mine was stuck like that, too.

The centre of Cambridge was a maze of old buildings the colour of half-sucked toffees and cold mashed potato, all fluffed up into domes and towers. The Prof said he'd give me a tour after lunch but first we'd go to his rooms.

Walking through the gates of St Saviour's was like stepping into one of those costume dramas Mum used to glue herself to on Sunday nights, only instead of girls in bonnets trying to bag themselves a husband it was full of students in jeans lugging books around. The Professor picked up his post from the porters' lodge, which was a kind of office to one side of the main gate, packed with keys, phones and pigeonholes. He introduced me a tubby bloke with wolf-man eyebrows and a bowler hat standing behind the desk.

'This is Albert Brewster, Joe, our head porter. Rules this place with a rod of steel.'

Albert looked me up and down. 'Pleased to meet you. And since you're a guest of the Professor's I'll turn a blind eye to the dog. Just this once.'

We traipsed across a couple of windy courtyards, through a maze of stone corridors and up these narrow steps to a massive book-lined room that smelled of leather, wood, paper, polish and coffee all stewed up for years and years. Through a half-open door at the back I could see a bedroom.

He told me to make myself at home. Yeah, right. As if any home I'd ever live in would have a carved wooden desk the size of a tennis court and those big pointy windows you get in churches, with a view straight on to the river. It didn't bother Oz. He went straight over and stretched himself out in front of the gas fire like he owned the place.

I put down Ivo's holdall and stood next to him, listening to the flames hiss and pop while the Prof fussed around making tea and telling me how glad he was I'd come. The mantelpiece was crowded with photos of Ivo and a dark-haired girl who looked just like him.

'Is that Bitsy?' I said.

He nodded, clearly pleased I'd remembered her name.

We talked a bit about Cambridge and him teaching philosophy and what exactly that meant, and he showed me some book he'd written about old coins and said he'd been collecting them since he was a kid. Neither of us mentioned Mum or Ivo till the Prof picked up the holdall and took out Ivo's notebook, holding it gently like it was a precious old relic.

'I'm so glad you brought me this, Joe. Somehow these blank pages seem to keep his potential alive. Is that stupid?' I shook my head. 'But I'd like you to keep his laptop.'

'Thanks, Professor,' I said. But he'd turned away as if it hurt too much to think about why it was going spare.

I waited, listening to the wind rattling the windows and watching his grip on the edge of the desk grow tighter. After a bit I said, 'That thing you said about Ivo's notebook. Yur . . . a friend said something like that about the way it hurts when someone you care about dies.'

The Prof's shoulders stiffened. 'Said what, Joe?'

'That the pain is good because it keeps the dead person alive in your heart.'

His head sank on to his chest, as if it had suddenly got too heavy to hold up. He stayed like that for a long time, with the notebook clasped in his hand and this sad feeling fluttering between us like it had a life of its own. After a while he made a tearing noise in his throat and put the notebook down.

'So, Ivo's laptop. Did you find anything interesting on it?'

Careful, Joe. Watch what you tell him. Take it slow and steady.

'There *was* something . . .'

The look he gave me was mostly pity but he couldn't hide the glint of curiosity in there as well.

'Ivo emailed this bloke at *The Times* and asked if he could write him an article about the KGB archives in Kiev — interviewing people whose names were in the files, hearing their side of what happened to them, stuff like that.'

The Professor pushed a few strands of longish grey hair off his face and gave a spot on the carpet a kind of faraway smile. 'Sounds like Ivo. He was marvellous at that sort of human story.' His watery blue eyes drifted back to me. 'But how does that back up your conspiracy theory?'

I took a breath. *OK, here goes.* 'What if he found something in the files, some secret information about KGB spies that someone powerful didn't want him to write about?'

The Professor raised his palm as if he was trying to push the idea away and said slowly and stiffly, 'Everything in those files has to be at least twenty years old. I think it very unlikely that anyone would kill to keep their contents quiet.'

'Unlikely. Not impossible.'

'Well, no,' he said wearily. 'Not impossible.'

I picked up the notebook. 'This writing, can you understand it?'

The Professor let out a sigh. 'No. It was Ivo's private shorthand. It made things much safer for him and his sources when he was reporting under cover.'

I turned the notebook towards him. 'Look at these dates. First one's the eleventh of February, last one's the day before the crash, the third of March. So this is all stuff he wrote in Ukraine.'

He nodded.

''So why bother writing it in code if he wasn't writing something secret?'

A tiny frown creased the Professor's forehead. I grabbed a pen and paper from his desk. 'OK, so think about it. Ivo goes to Kiev on the first of February. On the tenth of Feb he emails The Times about doing a story on the KGB archive. On the eleventh he starts investigating something and writing secret notes about it in this book. On the third of March, just as he's about to leave Ukraine, he has his laptop stolen. He flies home and buys a new one. The following night he goes to see my mum and they both get killed.'

I felt his eyes on me as I flicked through the notebook. 'Oh, yeah, and on the eleventh, right at the start of his investigation, he jots down these mobile numbers. They're probably contacts he was interviewing. Can we call them?'

'All right.' His voice was steady but his hand trembled as he handed me the phone.

I put it on speaker and rang the numbers. Each time I got a recorded voice telling me I'd dialled incorrectly. The Prof went over to his desk and tapped his computer.

'Try them again using the country code for Ukraine, that's 00380, and the one for Russia, which is 007.'

I looked up. 'You're not serious.'

'I'm afraid I am. It looks like someone in the Russian phone industry also had spies on the brain.' He tried to smile but didn't quite make it.

I dialled every combination – no luck.

'Maybe they're not mobile numbers at all,' he said, thoughtfully.

'Eleven digits, starting with an 0. What else are they going to be?'

Even as I said it I was getting this niggling feeling I'd seen another set of numbers just like them. Recently, too. I just couldn't think where. We tried writing them out, swapping the numbers for letters to see if they were some kind of code. All we got was a jumble of rubbish. The Prof heaved himself out of his chair. 'I don't know about you but my brain always works better on a full stomach. Come on. We're having lunch in the Senior Common Room. Better not be late.'

The Senior Common Room was like something out of Hogwarts; two long wooden tables down the middle and a lot of old portraits hanging round the walls. I was half expecting some wizened old gnome to hobble in and serve up stuffed swan and I was a bit miffed when it turned out to be a help-yourself choice of liver and bacon or breaded fish. I had the fish with rhubarb tart for afters. It was a bit like a posh school dinner except everyone was old and I had to keep stopping between mouthfuls so the Professor could introduce me to his mates. *This is my good friend, Joe Slattery.* I wish Mum could have seen me sitting there will all those crusty old professors. It would have made her year. She used to badger me all the time about going to university, getting a better life, not ending up like her. I was nodding, being polite and struggling to keep my elbows in, but all the time I was stressing about the questions I should ask Professor Lincoln. I was certain that if I only asked the right one I'd hit on the connection between Ivo, Mum and Yuri. But what that question was, well, that was anyone's guess.

After lunch the Prof took me and Oz on a tour of the town, pointing out a chapel the size of a cathedral, guiding me through narrow cobbled alleyways, dodging streams of students on bikes and letting me peer into a few more ancient colleges that looked like stately homes. I'm not usually into that kind of stuff but he made it pretty interesting, telling me stories about famous people who'd studied there and the wild stuff they'd got up to as students. Only instead of getting ASBOs they'd all gone on to become prime ministers, bankers and bishops. Even the ones who'd ended up as robbers, spies and murderers seemed to have got away with it, mainly because they were rich and posh. Just like Greville Clairmont. When I said that to the Professor he gave me a funny look.

'You're a bit young to know about the Clairmont murder,' he said.

We'd crossed a narrow stone bridge and as we walked along the river bank I let Oz off the lead and told the Prof about living in Saxted, my nan working for Norma Craig and how I'd had a peek inside Elysium when the cleaners were there. He was so interested that I got a bit carried away and nearly let it slip about Yuri. I stopped myself just in time.

'The murder was a huge story at the time,' he said. 'The papers talked about little else for weeks. And you're right. Clairmont *was* a Cambridge man.' He pointed to another big toffee-coloured building on the other side of the river. 'He was at Trinity, that college over there. Read History if I remember correctly.'

History!

The word lit a spark in my brain. It flickered for a couple of seconds then flared, lighting up a great big gap in my search of Ivo's laptop. I stopped dead.

The Prof turned and looked back at me. 'What's the matter?'

'I'm an idiot. I never checked Ivo's *browsing history*.'

We hurried back to St Saviour's and as soon as we got to the Professor's rooms I ran to Lincoln's laptop and hit the keys.

No triumph. Just a paralysing rush of fear. According to Ivo's browsing history, between the evening of 3 March and the morning of 4 March he'd searched the name

Sadie Slattery *nine* times. Half of me was desperate to know why. The other half was suddenly terrified of what I might find out.

I glanced up at the Professor, who was scanning the screen over my shoulder. He'd gone very pale. But he said, coolly and calmly, 'We mustn't get carried away. It's possible that Ivo just wanted to hear your mother sing.'

I wasn't even pretending to be cool or calm. 'Come on, Professor. I'm probably Mum's greatest fan and when she was on form her singing *was* really good. Just not good enough for anyone to get off a plane and start looking for her next performance before they'd had time to unpack. And anyway you don't go to the births, marriages and deaths register, the electoral roll or the vehicle licensing agency to find a music gig.'

I clicked through all the sites in the list till I got to the last one.

'Look at this, Professor,' I said. 'I don't think Ivo even knew that Mum *was* a singer till the morning of the crash.'

He peered closer. 'What makes you say that?'

'That's when he found her on the Trafalgar Arms events page.'

The Professor pulled off his glasses and rubbed his temples. 'This is all very unsettling, Joe. However it is hardly proof that my son and your mother were murdered.'

But as he paced up and down the room I could see his planet-sized brain was working overtime, turning over all the evidence we'd got so far.

All the way back to the station I was going mad trying

to match those numbers in Ivo's notebook with the hazy memory floating in my head. I was still thinking about it when the Prof grasped my shoulders, thanked me for coming and said we should meet up again as soon as he got back from a lecture he was giving in Edinburgh.

I boarded the train, put Oz under my seat and spread the list of numbers on the table in front of me. The door slammed. Maybe the sound jolted my brain or maybe it was seeing the paper against the brown plastic table that did it but a picture suddenly flashed in my head. Eleven black printed numbers on a white label . . . stuck on a brown cardboard box . . . on a still frame . . . of a YouTube clip.

'Stay there, Oz. Don't move.'

I barged back through the line of passengers coming down the aisle, ran for the door, jammed down the window and stuck my head out. The train was pulling out.

'Professor! I've got it! Those numbers. They're files! The KGB files Ivo looked at!'

A sudden smile cracked the sadness on his face. Raising his fists in a double thumbs-up he shouted into the wind, face flushed, eyes bright, hair whipping wildly round his head. 'Well done, Joe! I'll order copies and get them couriered.'

I waved till he was just a small lonely dot on the platform, and jumped when a tall heavy man brushed passed me lugging a suitcase. I stumbled to my seat, scared and excited, and lifted Oz on to my lap. He fell asleep pretty quickly and I was suddenly so exhausted it didn't take me long to drop off too.

This time the crash dream had a different twist. It was all about Ivo Lincoln smashing his car up trying to rescue Mum from Eddy Fletcher and her scabby life on Farm Street. The savage scream of brakes jolted me awake. As the train rolled into the station I caught my reflection in the window: a weedy kid in a cheap, washed-out hoodie. Mum had been planning to get me a new one. We'd have gone round the shopping centre, just her and me, trying on stuff we couldn't afford, having a laugh, pretending we were rich. That was never going to happen again. I felt totally lost. Mum's death might have strung a temporary bridge between my life and the posh bubble that people like Ivo and the Professor lived in, but our worlds would always be about a hundred million miles apart.

CHAPTER 9

I got back to Saxted to hear that Norma Craig had moved into Elysium that morning, Doreen was cooking her dinner that night, and I had to deliver it. Doreen wasn't sneering about Norma Craig's dodgy past now. In fact, from the fuss she was making you'd have thought she'd been asked to cater a royal wedding. It wasn't just the menu she was worried about. Oh, no. She was so petrified that I was going to 'let the side down' she made me have a shower while she shouted instructions through the bathroom door about what I had to say and do. How I'd got to stand up straight and look Norma in the eye and say *yes Miss Craig, no Miss Craig, anything you say Miss Craig* and take no notice if she was doddery and bad-tempered. And just in case Norma wanted to chat I had to keep to three safe topics: the weather, Doreen's amazing cooking, and my best subjects at school.

She'd also been shopping. When I got out of the shower she was in my room laying out a disgusting blue shirt, striped tie, tweed jacket, grey trousers and brown lace-up shoes.

'What's all this?' I said.

'I'm not having anyone delivering my food looking like an oik.'

Thanks, Doreen. At least I don't look like a whippet in a wig.

'Come on get dressed, we've got to leave in ten minutes.'

That's when I took my life in his hands, told her no way and threatened not to go. She backed down on the trousers and let me wear my black jeans. But I still had to wear the shirt, jacket and tie. *A tie!* And she wouldn't budge on the shoes. I felt like a total freak.

Doreen wasn't the only person in Saxted who'd got their knickers in a knot about Norma. She'd heard in the shop that there were reporters going door to door, trying to rake up gossip about the murder. We'd just loaded up the car when a sleazy-looking bloke came down the path, flashing a picture ID with 'Press' stamped across it, saying that he'd heard Doreen's mother had worked for the Clairmonts and did Doreen have any photos or stories she wanted to sell. Doreen slammed the car door in his face and drove off, which was a shame. I could have done with picking up a few investigation tips from a pro.

Doreen dropped me outside Elysium at exactly eight o'clock. She didn't seem in much of a hurry to leave, and watched from the car as the gates swung open and I walked down the floodlit drive. If she was hoping for a glimpse of Norma she was out of luck. A big bloke, with a golden tan, cropped blond hair and a sharp suit opened the front door. I wasn't sure if he was a butler or a bodyguard. Either way, I wouldn't want to upset him, which was a problem because, judging by the look on his face, I already had.

'I've got Miss Craig's dinner,' I said.

He paused, just long enough to make me think I'd got the wrong day, before forcing out the words, 'Come in.'

Talk about a makeover. The hall was cleaner than a disinfectant commercial, glittering with light and full of sweet-smelling flowers that made me sneeze. I glanced down the corridor to the cellar, wondering if there was much in the way of butlers and flower arrangements where Yuri had ended up.

Tan-man pushed open the door to the lounge and music flooded out; a bloke with a throaty voice singing an old song about windmills, spirals and half-forgotten dreams, I remembered Mum listening to it on one of her 'Hits of the sixties' CDs and singing along. The sound added to the creepy feeling I had that I was stepping back in time and made me think of Nan's photos and the way Elysium had looked in its pre-murder glory days.

I stood in the doorway and took it all in. The dust sheets and cobwebs had gone. The walls were painted, the leather couches cleaned, the curtains replaced, and the wooden floors polished. All the pictures of Norma had been dusted and straightened, and a row of little wall lights filled the whole place with a soft warm glow. Mum would have loved it.

A tall, slim woman was standing by the fireplace with her back to me, holding up a glass of wine that sparkled in the firelight. She turned slowly as I entered and, for a split second, it was like seeing a negative of the portrait behind her. Her hair was piled up in a similar way only it was white not black, and her long, floaty dress was black not white. The slanty eyes were just the same though, and they were scanning me inch by inch, just like Mum's used to do when she knew I was trying to hide something.

Norma Craig. She had to be well over sixty by now. No way did she look it. She must have seen I was shocked.

'What were you expecting? A crone?' Her voice cut the silence, husky and scornful.

'Er, no, Miss Craig.'

It looked like her lawyer had warned her I'd be doing the delivery because she didn't seem at all surprised to see a kid standing there with her dinner. I held up the heat-proof carry box. 'What shall I do with this?'

She lifted the glass and took a long sip. 'Raoul! Take him through.'

Raoul marched me across the hall to the dining room. Those Queens of Kleen had done a pretty good job in there as well. The chandeliers were glittering like disco balls, splashing blobs of light on to the walls and floor, and all the furniture had been polished to a gleaming shine. The big long table was set out with candles and wine, but laid with just one place. Sad or what? The double doors down the end of the room had been left open and I caught a glimpse of a sort of office with a big old-fashioned desk in the middle. But there was nothing retro about the massive computer, the bank of phones or the huge plasma screen she'd had installed.

Raoul took the lid off Doreen's salmon terrine and stood there holding out the dish like it was a used potty, and throwing me sneery looks.

'You got a problem?' I said.

'I have been cooking for Miss Craig for ten years and my food has always given complete satis . . .'

Norma swept in with a newspaper tucked under her arm. I turned to leave.

'I'd like you to stay!' she said.

I hovered at the other end of the table, not sure where I was s'posed to stand.

Raoul dumped a slice of terrine on her plate, and looked dead surprised when she flicked her wrist and told him to leave. He didn't like that at all. On his way out he glared at me like I was some devil child come to nick the silver. There was enough of it, that was for sure.

Norma Craig gave me a smile that was about as friendly as a crack in a tombstone. 'Joe Slattery, correct?'

I nodded. 'Yes, Miss Craig. I'm Doreen Trubshaw's nephew and . . .'

'Yes, my lawyer told me. I understand you're new to Saxted. How are you finding it?

'Um . . . fine, thanks.'

'Very different from your life in London, I should imagine.'

I put my hands in my pockets, feeling dead uncomfortable. 'Just a bit.'

'So what was it like?'

'What, Miss Craig?'

'Your life before you came here.'

What did she care? 'You know, ordinary.'

'Tell me about it. I crave a little diversion while I eat.'

So have your dinner in front of the telly like any normal person.

'Well?' She was staring at me, like I was in court or something.

I didn't see why I had to tell this total stranger the ins and outs of my life just because she was bored and I knew Doreen wouldn't be too pleased about it either. But I could tell that Norma was used to getting what she wanted, so I rattled on for a bit about Farm Street (leaving out the worst bits) and Mum's dreams of a proper singing career and how it was just the two of us after my father left . . .

It was like chucking petrol on a bonfire. She burst into a fit of fury, eyes blazing, nostrils flaring, chest heaving.

'Would you be that cruel, Joe Slattery? Would you trample on a woman's love and leave her to pick up the pieces?'

She was barking mad. I backed towards the door. 'Um . . .' What was I s'posed to say? I'd never even had a girlfriend, except for Chenisse Bains and I wasn't sure that one snog in the ASDA car park really counted as a meaningful relationship.

'Well?'

'I know this much, Miss Craig. I wouldn't run out on

someone and leave them with a kid. I saw what it did to my mum.'

That seemed to halt the meltdown.

'Was she very unhappy?'

'Off and on.'

'Betrayal leaves terrible scars.' She frowned and for a moment I thought she was actually feeling sorry for Mum. But no, five seconds later she was off on what was obviously her favourite subject: *herself*.

'Betrayal destroyed my life.'

Her fork clattered on to her plate and her whole body froze. Doreen's cooking had a similar effect on me but I got the feeling that food was the last thing on Norma's mind.

'Are you all right, Miss Craig?'

She just stared at the table. I was weighing up whether to make a dash for the door or try a comment about Doreen's 'amazing' terrine when she said in a hard voice.

'Do you know what happened out there in that hall-way?'

Whoa, this was way off Doreen's list of approved conversation topics.

'Um . . . kind of.'

'Can you imagine how it felt to discover that the man I loved had tried to kill me?'

'No, Miss Craig.'

'What kind of man could tell a woman he loved her while he was plotting to kill her in cold blood?' She didn't wait for an answer. 'I'll tell you what kind, a *monster*.' She spat the word and glared at me like I'd put

Clairmont up to it. 'A cold, pitiless monster. And they won't let me forget. Every few months there's a sighting of him or some cheap tabloid tries to dig over the ashes of my life.'

She flung the newspaper across the table. It was open at an article headlined 'NORMA CRAIG RETURNS TO HOUSE OF HORROR' above a picture of her and Clairmont looking young and glamorous. Her voice went flat and she stared into space as if she was repeating a speech she'd made a thousand of times before.

'The murder took place on a Friday, the day before our anniversary. At two that afternoon Greville went to a London florist and purchased a rare and beautiful orchid, one he knew I'd adore – then he went on to the bank and took out some family jewels for me wear at our anniversary ball the following evening.' Her eyes refocused and as they drilled into mine her voice switched from flat to angry. 'But it was all a front! A cover to hide his real intentions. Six hours later he returned home, put the orchid in the greenhouse then walked into this house and killed my housekeeper because he mistook her for me. And neither he nor the Clairmont emeralds have ever been seen since.'

Emeralds! My skin went hot then cold. I stepped back, shaking. *Emeralds like the bracelet, necklace and earrings I'd seen in Yuri's Oxo tin?* I tried to tell myself it was a coincidence, only it really didn't feel like one.

Cool it, Joe. Look away, breathe, sneeze, scratch, yawn, anything. Just don't let her see you're agitated.

Very slowly, an explanation I could deal with floated up through the scary mess of possibilities. Yuri must have found the emeralds hidden in the house. Yeah, that would be it. But if they really were the Clairmont emeralds and the cops caught him trying to flog them he'd be in a lot worse trouble than he was already. I tuned back in to Norma's voice and it was like she was talking to herself.

'Why did he do it? Was there corruption in the Clairmont blood? A streak of madness?' She let out a sob. 'He left me with nothing. No life at all.'

What was she on about? She was alive *and* healthy *and* rolling in money. Which was a lot more than could be said for her housekeeper or my mother. The way she whinged on about herself the whole time was really winding me up.

'The murder was pretty tough on Janice Gribben too,' I said. The words came spurting out before I could stop them but instead of going off on one she said very softly, 'Janice. My poor Janice.'

She was at it again! *Her* poor Janice.

'And terrible for her family,' I added.

She looked up. 'She didn't have any family.'

I couldn't stop thinking about that tiny blurred photo of Janice in the papers and the way the press had practically ignored her, just like they'd practically ignored Mum. It really riled me.

'Just because people aren't famous it doesn't mean they don't matter,' I said. 'You should have stepped in and given the papers a decent photo of her.'

She stared into space, shaking her head. 'I didn't have one. Janice hated having her photo taken. The minute she saw a camera she'd disappear.'

It was like Janice Gribben had never existed. No family to miss her, no grave to put a headstone on, not even a photo for anyone to glance at and go *oh yeah, that's Janice, I remember her.*

Norma's eyes filled with tears. 'Janice was devoted to me. Don't you worry about a thing, Miss Craig,' she used to say. 'You concentrate on being beautiful. Leave the rest to me.' And I did. Everything from the food and the guest lists to running the staff. She used to come to my room at night to lay out my clothes for the next day and we'd talk and talk. I had no secrets from Janice.'

I couldn't take much more of Norma Craig's crazy mood swings. I wanted out of there. I glanced at the food Raoul had left on the sideboard.

'Your dinner's getting cold, Miss Craig. Doreen's done you sautéed duck. She said to tell you that the um . . . flavours in the sauce are . . . um . . . a "subtle fusion of—"'

'What do I care about food? Guilt drains the pleasure out of everything – eating, thinking, even dreaming.'

If Norma didn't fancy the duck I was tempted to ask if I could take it back for Oz, but she looked so miserable I said, 'You can't blame yourself for the murder.'

'Murder?' Surprised, she looked up at me with those big slanty eyes. 'Believe me, Joe, there are far more inhuman crimes than murder.'

I didn't have the nerve to ask what she meant but to stop her working herself into a state again I said, 'My mum wrote this song once about regretting it when you mess up and how people should try to be understanding about it even if they can't totally forgive you.'

Norma mulled that over. 'Did your mother have many regrets?'

'A few.'

She shook her head and tears splashed down her face. 'I've lost the only chance I ever had for forgiveness or understanding. Regrets are all I have. That's what happens when you do something truly terrible. The need for secrecy poisons your whole life. The lies, the pretence, the guilt, they eat away at you until there's nothing left. Half a lifetime ago I turned my back on this house because of Greville Clairmont and I hoped that by coming back I might have a chance of salvaging just a little of what might have been. Of picking up the pieces of my life.'

She'd lost me, totally.

'Er . . . so why don't you go out, have some fun, look up some old mates?' It was the kind of thing I used to say to Mum when Eddy was giving her grief. I got the same reaction.

A single tear trickled down her cheek. 'If only it were that simple.'

Her eyes fixed on mine. I shifted my feet and gave her a nervous smile. Her whole body stiffened and her face went stonier than one of her statues.

Now what had I done?

'I'd like you to leave now,' she said. Then she got up and walked out without saying another word.

CHAPTER 10

I ran into the hall in time to hear the last echoes of Norma's high heels clicking up the stairs. Raoul was waiting for me, holding the front door open and working his jaw like a boxer before a fight. I didn't hang around to say goodbye. Sprinting down the drive, I made a dash through the slowly opening gates and into the woods.

As far as wacky experiences go, that visit to Elysium had to be up there with the wackiest. But compared to tracking Yuri down and finding out if Ivo Lincoln's visit to the KGB archive was the key to Mum's death it was just a sideshow. So why did I feel like I was falling apart? Maybe crazy was catching, or maybe finding out about the emeralds was sending me places I didn't want to go.

I darted round the back of Laurel Cottage, ran straight to the shed and buried my face in Oz's warm, musty fur. I wanted Mum. I wanted to her to tell me not to worry because Norma Craig was just a batty old woman who liked winding people up.

'Joe? Are you in there?'

The shed door swung open. I looked up. It was Doreen. Oz padded forward and took a cautious sniff at her hand, jerking back again when she batted him away,

'I expected you back ages ago. I've been waiting to hear how it went. What took you so long?'

'Miss Craig, she er . . . wanted me to hang around while she ate.'

Her eyes flashed. 'Did she enjoy the food? Come on what did she think about the terrine?'

'She . . . she said it was great.'

'Details, Joe, I want to know *exactly* what she said, what she was wearing, what the house looked like. My other clients are all *dying* to know.'

What about your reputation for discretion, Doreen? And anyway I didn't get it. If she was that interested why hadn't she delivered the food herself?

'Come on. In the house. I'm freezing to death out here.'

What do you think it's like for Oz, stuck in the shed, all night every night?

He pawed my leg and whined when I got up. 'I'll be back in a bit,' I whispered. 'This won't take long. Not if I can help it.'

I could have killed for a burger and a bit more quiet time with Oz. Instead I had to make do with a slice of goats' cheese quiche and the third degree from Doreen.

But I had to be careful. She'd have gone mad if she knew what had really happened at Elysium. So I had a go at filling her in on Norma's hairdo, outfit and choice of cushion covers, and pretended that she'd loved the duck and we'd chatted about the weather. I was glad I didn't have to describe the look Norma had given me just before she told me to leave. I'd never have found the words.

My dream that night was full of emeralds, Oxo tins, and Norma and Mum giving me the same guilt probe stare while I told them over and over that I hadn't done anything. But the ending was just the same, the oncoming 4x4 and the screeching grind of metal. I woke up yelling for Mum, just like the time I lost her in Tesco's when I was about five. What I wanted more than anything was the rush of relief I'd got when she came flying down the biscuit aisle to find me. But no one was going to be coming for me now. Well, no one except Oz.

When I finally made it downstairs and into the garden, he came shooting out of the shed so fast he practically did a back flip off the end of his chain. It must have really hurt him. It was a good thing Doreen was out or I'd have wrapped that stupid chain right round her scrawny neck just so she knew how it felt. I unclipped him and headed down the main street towards the river, trying to think up interesting ways of making Doreen suffer. I'd just got her strung up over a boiling vat of fish tagine, screaming for mercy, when I realised I'd turned off by the pub and doubled back towards the graveyard. Who knows why? Maybe I was feeling guilty about all the lying and stealing

I'd been doing for Yuri and wanted to square it with Mum. Maybe I missed her so much I couldn't help it. Anyway, even from the road, I could see there was something not right about her grave.

I jumped over the fence and stared down at the massive wreath lying there. It was the size of a tractor tyre; all white rosebuds and bits of ivy, mixed in with that pink and yellow stuff that smells really sweet, what's it called . . . honeysuckle. It must have cost an arm and a leg. It had to be a mistake, meant for some other dead person. One with rich relations who cared. I snatched up the card: 'SADIE RIP'.

The ground fell away, taking my stomach with it. This was either a sick joke, or some kind of warning – you know, like in the movies when the mob kills someone then sends a truckload of flowers round to the church to make sure everyone knows it was them. I hurled that wreath so hard it bounced off the gate, then I ran over and stamped on it till all that was left was a tangle of wire and a squashy mess of petals. Did it make me feel better? No. It didn't. And if I hadn't realised it before, I realised it now. The only thing that was ever going make me feel even the tiniest bit better was catching Mum's killer.

I got this tight, prickly feeling on the back of my head. I turned round and caught a bloke watching me from a silver Volvo parked on the grass verge. He was scratching his stubble and talking into his mobile. He must have seen me going crazy. I didn't care. He should mind his own business. I glared at him. The way he stared back unnerved me. After a bit he pocketed his phone, slipped the car into gear and slid off down the road. I waited for the uneasiness to drain away, annoyed when it hung around like scum at the bottom of the bath.

I walked back to Mum's grave and smoothed away the mark left by the wreath. I had to find Yuri. Only he could tell me if the 'bad people' trying to silence him were the same ones who'd silenced Mum and Lincoln. And only he could tell me why. But I wasn't going to find him by hanging around Saxted trashing over-the-top floral tributes. I had to go to London. That's where Yuri had been headed and that's where Mum had died. I'd start with the Trafalgar Arms. So what if the thought of walking through that door sent a thousand volts of pain through my guts? There was just a chance that one of the bar staff had overheard what Mum and Ivo Lincoln had been talking about.

I was dying to go straight up to my room and start packing but Doreen had other ideas. The minute I walked in she sprang out of the kitchen yelling.

'I just got back from the farmer's market and what did I find? The house empty and the back door hanging wide open. I knew you couldn't be trusted.'

I spun round to check the door.

'There's nothing wrong with the lock,' she snapped. 'Plain thoughtless, that's what you are. Just like your mother. It's a wonder we weren't burgled. Anyone could have waltzed off with the television, all my jewellery, George's computer and heaven knows what else. And as if that wasn't enough you've been traipsing mud all over the house. Don't deny it. There were footprints in the hall, on the stairs and in our bedroom, when I've expressly forbidden you to go in there. So what have you got to say for yourself?'

How about It *wasn't me, Doreen, I'm not that stupid?* But she'd never have believed me so I mumbled I was sorry and raced upstairs, praying that Ivo's laptop would still be there.

'I haven't finished with you, young man!'

I burst into my bedroom. The laptop had gone. It only took one look in the drawers to see they'd been searched by someone who'd been nowhere near as sneaky about it as Doreen. I was sweaty and shaking. Maybe it was kids. Maybe they'd slipped into the house on the off chance and only bothered with the room that had kids' stuff in it. Yeah, that would explain everything; the mud, the rummaging and the fact that none of Doreen and George's things had been nicked. There were just two small problems with that. One – I'd definitely locked the door when I went out, and two – there was no sign of a break-in. Whoever had got into Laurel Cottage had made a neat, professional job of picking the lock and gone straight for Lincoln's laptop. It had to be someone who'd been hanging round the village, waiting for me to go out. The prickle in my scalp flared up again and fluttered down my spine. Someone like that shifty bloke who'd been watching me in the graveyard.

'I said, I haven't finished with you!'

I went back downstairs, trying to convince myself I was imagining things and that Doreen had faked the whole thing to give herself an excuse to turf me out.

Either way, my immediate future wasn't looking great – I'd either be spending it in care or dodging the gangsters who were trying to stop me discovering Lincoln's secrets.

Close up, Doreen's anger seemed pretty genuine. I mean, keeping her face the colour of cherryade and making a noise like a leaky piston every time she looked my way can't have been easy. She was working herself up to have another go at me when the phone rang. She grabbed the receiver. Her voice changed quicker than a flicked switch.

"Oh, Mr Pritchard. Hello. Joe tells me that everything went very well last night . . ."

'What?' Her eyes locked on to mine like a couple of heat-seeking lasers. 'There must be a misunderstanding . . .'

'But I . . .'

'Supposing I . . .'

'I realise that, but . . .'

'Yes . . . I'll send my invoice.'

She slammed down the phone, the cherryade flush took on a nasty tinge of Ribena and her breathing went so weird I was scared she was having a heart attack.

'What's up?'

'Don't you play innocent with me. That was Norma Craig's lawyer calling to terminate her contract.'

This was all I needed.

'Do you have any idea of the trouble George's business is in or how much a contract like that meant to us?'

'It's not my fault. I did everything you said but she's insane.'

'Are you trying to blame my cooking? I've never had a

complaint, not in twenty years of catering. It must have been you. Turning up in jeans and talking like a lout. I knew it would end in disaster.'

'So why d'you make me do it then?'

'You think I wanted to? It was her idea. Some crazy notion about wanting a fresh young face around the place. But you had to mess it up, didn't you, because you're a selfish, inconsiderate taker just like your . . .'

'Don't you *dare* say another word about my mum. Don't you *dare*! You think you're better than she was but you're not. You're just a dried-up snobby old cow who doesn't care about anyone but yourself. I don't know how George puts up with you.'

'I won't be spoken to like that in my own house. Go to your room. Now!'

'Don't worry. I'm off. And you know what? You can stick your stinking house *and* your stupid rules. I'm going back to London.'

'Back to that sleazy boyfriend of your mother's? Last I heard, he didn't want anything to do with you. And I can see why.'

'I'd rather sleep on the streets than stay here!'

'That's just where you're headed, Joe Slattery, and don't come grovelling to me when you end up in trouble.'

I ran upstairs and started stuffing clothes into my rucksack and shoving everything else into a carrier. By the time I'd finished, both bags were bulging but I wasn't going to leave any of Mum's stuff behind for Doreen to chuck out. She was right about Eddy, though. If I turned up at our old flat he'd slam the door in my face. I'd stay with Bailey and his brother Jackson – they'd see me all right for a bit. After that, who knew where I'd end up? I didn't care. Right now the only thing that mattered was catching Mum's killer.

CHAPTER 11

I was edgy all the way to London, trying to shake off the feeling I was being watched. Trouble is, once you start worrying about something like that everyone you see looks dodgy. By the time I got to London I only had three quid left of the twenty George had given me. I knew I should have saved the fare and walked from the tube to the Trafalgar Arms but I took the bus, reckoning it was the best way to avoid the crash site. Wrong. When the driver pulled up at the stop before the pub, my gaze had already clamped on to the manky bunches of flowers hanging off the lamp post in crinkly cellophane wrappers. Even when I wrenched my eyes away they flew straight up the narrow concrete column to the CCTV camera that had videoed the accident. The old couple standing beside me stepped back as if I'd made a weird noise or something so I grabbed Oz, got off and ran the rest of the way.

I'd sat on the steps of that pub enough times as a kid with a Coke and a bag of crisps waiting for Mum and Eddy, but I'd never been inside. I hadn't missed much: red vinyl seats, a sad-looking stage, a few old codgers sitting round the telly watching darts and a fat landlord with dark wiry hair and small suspicious eyes who looked like a bear that'd just been woken up from hibernation and wasn't too pleased about it.

'No kids or dogs in the bar,' he grunted, without taking his eyes off the TV.

I was shaking and it was making me stammer. 'S . . . sorry . . . I . . . my mum . . . I'm S . . . Sadie Slattery's son.'

His little eyes slid round to look at me. 'I've already paid Eddy what she was owed.'

No danger of the old *sorry-for-your-loss* arm-squeezing routine then.

I couldn't let him get to me. 'I . . . I'm not here about money. I . . . I want to talk to whoever was behind the bar the night of the crash.'

His eyes swivelled back to the TV. He opened his mouth and bellowed, 'Shauna!'

A voice yelled back that she was busy. He shouted again, crosser this time, and kept it up until a fair-haired woman, younger than him but not by much, wearing a red dress, a lot of make-up and yellow rubber gloves stuck her head through the door behind the bar.

'Someone to see you,' the landlord said, working a cocktail stick between his front teeth. 'Sadie's kid.'

It was the woman's turn to look at me. Her face softened.

102

'Can I have a word?' I sounded like a detective off one of the cheesy cop shows Mum used to watch.

She nodded towards the back. I whistled to Oz and squeezed past the landlord, who barely shifted his baggy backside to make room.

'Don't mind Don,' she said, leading the way upstairs. 'He's always in a mood in the mornings. Cuppa?'

'Thanks.'

The kitchen in their flat was bright and cheerful after the gloom of the bar, and loads cleaner. Oz was squinting up at her with his tongue hanging out. As she filled the kettle she poured him a bowl of water.

'What's this about, Joe?'

'How do you know my name?'

'Sadie's been singing here for years. Course I know your name, she talked about you often enough. I'd have come to the funeral only Eddy left it to the last minute to tell me when it was and Don couldn't spare me from the bar.' She took a couple of tea bags out of a jar. 'She was a good woman, your mum. A good friend and a good singer.'

I could see she was about to get teary so I said quickly, 'I want to know about that bloke Lincoln who was driving the car. What happened? Did he just go up to her after the gig or had they been chatting before?'

'Why do you want to know?'

I gave her the line I'd prepared. 'It's weird she was in his car when she never got lifts from strangers. I just wondered if there was anything . . . going on.'

She closed the door. 'How do you get on with Eddy?'

'I don't.'

She curled her lip. 'He's big mates with my Don. Personally, I never worked out what Sadie saw in him.'

I nodded, though from what I'd seen of Don, Shauna and Mum were running neck and neck in the dud bloke stakes.

She dropped her voice. 'It makes me sick the way he comes in here accusing your mum of everything under the sun when I know for a fact that the only time she ever clapped eyes on Ivo Lincoln was the night of the crash.'

'How do you know that?'

She eyed the door and leant across the table. 'Because he rang the pub that morning and it was me who took the call.'

I tipped forward on my seat, heart beating fast.

'What did he want?'

She frowned and looked down.

'Please, Shauna. Mum used to tell me everything; she'd have wanted me to know.'

She closed her eyes and sighed. 'All right. He gave me his number, said he was a journalist and he wanted Sadie to call him urgently. I got straight on to her and told her she must have come into money. To tell you the truth we had a good laugh about it. Anyway, when she rang him back he said it was too important to be discussed over the phone. She was a bit suspicious and arranged to meet him here after the gig where she knew there'd be lots of people around, and we looked his photo up online so we'd know if it really was him. There was a big crowd in that night but I spotted him just as the band started playing. He was nice-looking, very polite, took his pint over to that table in the corner and waited till Sadie had finished her set. Then he bought her a drink, they talked for a while and he showed her something . . .'

'What was it?'

'I couldn't really see from the bar but she had her head down for a long time like she was looking at it. Then I'm pretty sure she put it in her bag. Whatever he was telling her it must have been interesting because she barely said a word, just sat there listening.'

That didn't fit with my idea of a journalist. 'Are you sure he wasn't asking her questions?'

'Didn't look like it.'

'And you've no idea what he said?'

'I caught her up as they were leaving and asked if she'd inherited a million. She was white as a sheet and said no and made me swear not to tell anyone about Lincoln, 'specially not Eddy. Said she needed time to think things through. Then they left and . . . well, you know the rest.'

'Think what things through?'

'I've no idea.'

'And she only had one drink?'

'A glass of wine. I don't know who told the papers she was tipsy but it wasn't true. Still, I kept my promise to Sadie and till now I haven't told anybody what really happened.'

'I'd give anything to know what Lincoln told her.'

'Whatever it was, pet, it can't make any difference now. If you ask me, we should let Sadie and her secrets rest in peace.' She got up from the table. 'I'm going to grab a quick sandwich, do you want one?'

'Yeah, thanks.'

'Ham and cheese, all right?'

'Great.'

Shauna might have blown my Mum-giving-Ivo-information theory but she'd confirmed that Lincoln had tracked her down to talk about something important. Shauna passed me a sandwich and topped up our teas.

'It's a shame Eddy hasn't managed to get in touch with Lizzie. Who is she, an old friend?'

I bit into the sandwich. 'Who?'

She looked flustered. 'Didn't Eddy tell you?'

I shook my head.

'The fireman, the one who . . . cut your mum out of the car. He went round your flat the day after the crash. I thought you were there.'

'Me and Oz went down the canal. I couldn't stick Eddy shouting and carrying on. What did this fireman want?'

'To say that . . . that . . . when he got there Sadie was still conscious. He said she grabbed his hand and said something over and over . . . like it was really important.'

I got this spasm in my throat that made it hard to speak. 'What was it?'

'"Tell Joe and Lizzie."'

'Tell us what?'

'That's it. Just, "Tell Joe and Lizzie."'

'The fireman . . . he must've heard her wrong. Mum didn't even know anyone called Lizzie.'

'You sure? He got your name right.'

Suddenly I was seeing Mum trapped in the wreckage,

reaching out to a stranger, struggling to send me a last, gasped-out message and running out of life before she could finish it. *What was it, Mum? What were you trying to tell me?* I dropped my head on the table, feeling the burning taser pain give way to a dizzying drop into endless nothing.

'I'm sorry, Joe. I could wring Eddy's neck for not telling you.'

I felt her hand on my head and pulled away. 'If he finds her, can you give me a call?'

I grabbed her phone pad and scribbled down Bailey's number.

'All right pet,' she said, frowning. 'But as for the rest of it, as I said, maybe it's best to let things lie.'

Don started yelling at her to come down and bottle up.

I said goodbye, slipped out into the street and started walking to Farm Street. *Lizzie, Liz, Elizabeth.* I felt a stab of jealousy, like ice on a tooth. *Who is she, Mum? And why was her name the last word you ever spoke?*

CHAPTER 12

After posh, uptight Saxted, the estate looked even scruffier and crazier than before. Eight identical low-rise blocks slashed with stained concrete walkways, arranged around a pathetic excuse for a play area, and surrounded by a sea of overflowing wheelie bins. Whoever picked the name Farm Street must have been having a laugh. The only crop growing round there was the weed Bailey's brother Jackson sold by the ounce. Though you won't catch me knocking Jackson Duval. If it wasn't for him I'd have been diced, skewered and bar-bequed the minute we moved in. And now I needed his help again.

Oz was scampering around, barking and lifting his leg against every bin bag in sight. He was ecstatic to be back and I have to admit, the thought of swapping Doreen's company for Bailey's was starting to cheer me up too. Me and Bailey first got to know each other because we both spent our lunch breaks in the ICT suite. Only unlike me he wasn't hiding, he just liked computers. I'd been at the school a couple of days, having the usual trouble settling in, when this other new kid, Trevor Mitchum, decided to show the world how hard he was by dropping by and giving us a hard time. The downside was that me and Bailey got well and truly thrashed. The upside was that we shared our pain and became friends. That night Jackson and a couple of his crew went round to welcome Trevor to the area. There were lots of upsides to that. Trevor got to meet the neighbours, learned not to throw his weight around till he'd checked who he was messing with, and never bothered us again.

I'd been keeping a constant look out for a silver Volvo and a man with stubble and I went on running my eyes around as I walked through the estate. The lights were on in our lounge which meant Eddy was up there with his mates, drinking beer and dropping fag ash on Mum's cushions. A woman with long dark hair and a brown coat hurried past. For a minute I could have sworn it was Mum. I shouted, '*Hey!*'

The woman turned. She looked nothing like Mum. I felt stupid as well as robbed. I started to run. Suddenly I could see Mum everywhere – crossing the car park, climbing the stairs, heading down the walkway. I lurched into a stairwell doubled over by a blast of taser pain that was filling my head with breathy gasps of *Tell Joe and Lizzie* and pitching me into nothingness. I don't long how I leant against the wall breathing fast before the pain got bearable. Hoping no one I knew had seen me acting weird I peered out and looked around for Oz. He was way off, heading towards our old flat. He thought we were going home. I whistled and slapped my leg.

'Oz, c'mon. Here boy! This way.'

He skidded to a halt, turned on one paw and bounded back, swerving straight past me and making a dash for Bailey's flat.

Obviously it wasn't *actually* Bailey's flat, he shared it with Jackson. For ages after their mum married her loser boyfriend and went back to Haiti, it was a right tip, but ever since Jackson's girlfriend Danielle and their kid Rikki had moved in, things had improved.

Music was blasting through the walls. I had to knock hard and shout through the letterbox before Danielle opened up, joggling Rikki on her hip. She ruffled my hair like I was about five, which was rich considering she was only a few years older than me.

I pushed her hand off. 'Hey, Danielle. Do you know anyone on the estate called Lizzie who might have been a friend of Mum's?'

She shook her head.

'Can you ask around for me?'

'Sure,' she said and went back to her mates, who were sitting round the kitchen table doing each other's nails.

Bailey was asleep on the couch in the front room. He was a bit taller and chubbier than me and though Danielle was always trying to smarten him up and get him to wear cooler glasses he preferred scruffy jeans and his old glasses, even though one of the lenses was chipped. Oz jumped on his head. He looked round, gave me this feeble biff on the arm and wheezed out a croaky, 'Hey.'

'What's up with you?'

'Another stupid infection.'

Bailey reached for his asthma inhaler and I watched him shake it, squirt and suck. He didn't look good. His skin was ashy and his breathing had this worrying rattle to it that I hadn't heard in a while. I mean, I was used to him having bad days but now and then they get scary, like the time a couple of years back when he collapsed on the stairs of our block. Thing was, he was home alone and it was Mum who found him and got him to hospital. They said it was touch and go. If she'd turned up ten minutes later … well, who knows?

Jackson never said a word of thanks, didn't need to because that's when he started looking out for Mum as well as me, and her life on Farm Street notched up from the total pits to almost OK. No more rubbish dumped outside our flat, respect from the hoodies on the walkway and a fistful of fivers from the kids who chucked a ball through our window. 'Course, Eddy thought he'd lucked out and started throwing his weight around till he discovered that Jackson's helping hand didn't actually stretch as far as him.

'Why's your phone turned off?' Bailey said.

'I gave it away.'

'Who to?'

'This old tramp. Lend us yours a sec.'

I rang St Saviour's and left Bailey's number on the

Prof's voicemail, telling him it was the best way to reach me for the next couple of days.

Bailey gave me one of his sideways looks. 'Who's Professor Lincoln?'

'Long story. It's kind of why I'm here.'

'I'm listening.' He heaved himself up. ''Cos I swear, boredom's going to kill me way before asthma gets a chance.'

So I told him everything. I even showed him Nan's scrapbook and told him all about Mum's meet with Lincoln in the pub. Halfway through he reached for his glasses and laptop and started hitting the keys.

'What you doing?'

'Thinking. Go on.'

He went on typing even after I'd finished talking, stopping now and then to ask a question or push his glasses up his nose and squint at the screen. Finally he said, 'You're right, you gotta find Yuri.'

It was weird. Hearing someone else say Yuri's name made him seem realer. 'Yeah,' I said. 'And I reckon once he got to London he'd be looking to get help from other Ukrainians who aren't too friendly with the cops. I was kind of hoping Jackson might have some contacts in that area . . .'

'Jackson's got contacts in all areas. But he likes to keep them personal.'

'Is he around?'

'In his office.'

I headed for the door.

'I wouldn't if I were you.'

'It's important.'

He looked up. When he saw I was deadly serious he nodded and reached for Nan's scrapbook.

Jackson's 'office' was a flat on the top of the opposite block that had been gutted by fire. Some older kids took it over till Jackson decided it had the makings of an ideal business premises. He wasn't a big fan of sunshine or nosy neighbours so the boarded-up windows suited him fine. Mum would have had a fit if she'd known I was even thinking of going in there. I mean, she was really grateful for the way Jackson had helped her out and everything but there were large parts of his life she didn't want to know about. What went on in that office was one of them.

I crossed the play area and climbed the stairs, slowing down as I turned on to the top floor. I stood in front of the office door feeling like I'd pulled on someone else's skin and it didn't fit. Oz looked up at me, expectant.

'OK,' I whispered. 'Here goes.'

I took a breath and rapped on the charred woodwork. I knew one of Jackson's runners would be checking me out through a spy hole so I stepped back to give them a clear view. After about five minutes I heard a couple of bolts scraping then the door opened about two inches. This tall skinny kid they call Blu-ray was staring through the gap. I'd never liked him much. He was sixteen going on twenty-five with a bar-code eyebrow, heavy gold chains and a swagger like a walk-on in a gangsta movie. He was always sucking up to Jackson, trying to show him how smart he was.

'Watchoo want?' he snarled.

'I gotta see Jackson. It's important.'

He shut the door in my face. I waited another five minutes then it opened and Blu-ray jerked his head towards the gloomy hallway. I stepped inside and followed him into the back room. The only light piercing the smoke came from a couple of bare bulbs and a few holes in the window panels where the bolts had come loose. Someone had done a bit of cleaning up since the fire, scrubbed the soot off the walls and put in chairs, a table, an old plastic couch and a fridge. Half a dozen blokes I didn't like the look of, broke off a noisy discussion when I walked in. From the way they were glaring they weren't overly happy about the interruption.

Jackson rocked back in his chair, gold tooth and diamond earring glinting. You could see he was Bailey's brother but his face was thinner and harder. He had on a black tracksuit and his hair was braided and tied back.

'What you want, Joe? I'm busy.'

'I need to see you. It's important. And private.'

The glares got harder. Waving down the rumble of mutters, Jackson swung his feet off the table and stood up. 'This better be good.'

He wasn't tall or broad but he had this way of making everyone around him seem smaller than they actually were. Me included. He took me through to what was left of the kitchen and leant against the wall, arms folded.

'So?'

'You're the only person I know who can help me.'

'Why's that?'

'You've got contacts . . . connections ...' His eyes

114

narrowed. I could feel my face growing hot and my voice going stuttery. 'With people who . . . know what's going on.'

'And?'

'You've got to help me find someone.'

'He got a name?'

'Yuri.'

'Yuri what?'

'I don't know. But he's mixed up in some bad stuff and he's on the run.'

'Who from?'

'Someone who wants to kill him.'

His eye bored into mine.

'Why you want him?'

'He's got some information I need.'

''Bout what?'

''Bout what happened to Mum.'

The look he was giving me made me squirm. 'Meaning?'

I stared straight back, didn't even blink. 'Maybe the crash wasn't an accident.'

He lifted one eyebrow. 'Why you think that?'

For the second time that day I blurted it out in one long blabbery stream: Ivo Lincoln visiting Ukraine, coming back and searching for Mum, Yuri being Ukrainian, on the run from people trying to kill him, and coming to London to look for Ivo. When I'd finished Jackson didn't say a word, just went on looking at me.

'Don't you believe me?' I said.

'Doesn't matter what I believe. You don't want to go

messing with no Ukes. They're trouble. Big trouble.'

'If the crash wasn't an accident Yuri's my only chance of finding out who did it and why. If he's in London you must know someone who can help me find him.'

'OK. Supposing you find this Yuri and he says you're right about the crash. What you gonna do about it?'

'I just got to know the truth, Jackson. It's burning me up. I need you to hook me up with someone who's in with the Ukrainians, someone who can do a bit of asking around without looking suspicious.'

Jackson looked up. Blu-ray was at the door. Who knows how long he'd been there. 'Erroll Potts wants you to call him. Says it's urgent.'

Jackson nodded and turned back to me.

Blu-ray went on hovering in the doorway, eager to muscle in. 'Believe it, Joe. Those Ukes ain't scared of nothing. Hey, Jackson, you remember that time—'

Jackson gave him a death stare. 'Shut it, Blu-ray.'

'But Jack—'

'I said. Shut it.'

Blu-ray slunk off. Jackson leant his face close to mine. 'You drop this, Joe. Right now.'

'I'm doing it for Mum. Don't you care who killed her?' I'd blurted it out before his glare could choke off the words.

'You think she'd want you dead, too?'

'I have to know who did it.'

'Listen up, Joe. I look after my own, you know that. But you do anything stupid, I can't help you. Now I got a meeting going on.'

I fumbled in my jeans for the tie-clip and thrust it into his hand. 'What about this? Can you sell it for me?'

Jackson held it to the light and I saw his whole face change.

'Where you get this?' he said.

'Yuri gave it me. It's real, isn't it?'

'Looks like it.' He handed it back. 'Piece like that going to get the wrong people asking questions.'

'But I need money.'

He chucked me a couple of tenners. 'Now get out of here.'

It wasn't anywhere near enough but it was better than nothing. I put the tie-clip back in my pocket and made for the door. I felt his hand grip my shoulder. He turned me around.

'Take it from me, Joe. If this Yuri's running from trouble, he don't want to be found. Not by you. Not by anyone.'

I dumped a box of KFC on Bailey's knees and reached for the ketchup.

'Where's Danielle?'

'Round her mum's.' He tore off a strip of chicken and folded it into his mouth. 'How'd it go with Jackson?'

I gave him the bad news.

'Told you.'

'One thing's for sure, his strop with Blu-ray proves he's had dealings with Ukrainians.'

Bailey flicked me a look and stopped eating.

'What?' I said.

'Nothing.'

'What d'you know that you're not telling?'

'Nothing. I was just thinking about that house, Elysium. Yuri was hiding there. Your nan used to work there. That's way too weird to be random.'

I was getting angry. 'Don't lie. What were you really thinking?'

'I told you.'

'Bailey, I'm doing this for Mum. And you owe her!'

I felt bad saying it, but I was desperate.

'OK. OK.' He crossed his arms and glared at me. He hated being forced into things but he knew he didn't have a choice. 'There is a Ukrainian Jackson did some business with. Viktor something.'

'All right. Now we're getting somewhere.'

'You don't want to go near him. He came round once, brought a couple of heavies with him and left a load more outside patrolling the walkway. They freaked Danielle out.'

'Where's he live?'

'Acton . . . Shepherd's Bush, I don't know, somewhere out west. Jackson made me stay in my room but I heard this Viktor going on about his restaurant serving the best Ukrainian food in London and how Jackson should take Danielle over to try it. But the restaurant's not how he makes his money. He's into all sorts.'

'So I'll find the restaurant and go see him,' I said.

'I don't think so.'

I picked up his laptop and started tapping. 'There's three Ukrainian restaurants in London and only one in West London. It's called the Besedka.' I scanned the screen.

'The owner's V. Kozek. That him?'

'Yeah,' he said gloomily. 'Viktor Kozek. But honestly, Joe, someone like that, you can't just—'

'I'm going, Bailey.'

'What if Jackson finds out?'

'I gotta chance it. What else can I do?' I closed the search and clicked through the pages he'd got up. I'd only been away for an hour and he'd already found loads of stuff about Ivo Lincoln and Norma Craig.

'What's this clip?'

'A report off yesterday's news about Norma Craig going back to Saxted. Have a look.'

I pressed play and felt a shiver of recognition as old photos of Elysium, Norma and Clairmont flashed on to the screen.

'Sixties icon Norma Craig has returned to Elysium, the home she abandoned over three decades ago when her husband, Lord Greville Clairmont, was accused of murder. For five years they held court in their luxurious modernist mansion, playing host to a glamorous circle of writers, politicians, musicians, scientists, actors and royalty. However the party came to an abrupt end when Greville Clairmont bludgeoned their housekeeper, Janice Gribben, to death in the darkened hallway mistaking her for his wife.

'The couple's gardener told police he saw Clairmont stashing the body into his Mercedes and the car was discovered the next day, abandoned on the cliffs at Dover. However, despite a lengthy search of the coastal waters Janice Gribben's body was never found. Soon afterwards

Norma Craig left Britain for Switzerland where she has led a reclusive existence ever since.

'And as for Greville Clairmont – on the day of the murder he literally vanished without trace. The man who led the initial murder hunt and followed up every alleged sighting was Inspector Keith Treadwell of Scotland Yard. Now retired, he's here with me now.'

The shot cut to a washed-out old guy with deep wrinkles all across his forehead as if he frowned a lot.

'Keith Treadwell, what do you think of the speculation that Norma Craig has returned to Britain because Clairmont is here and wants to make his peace with her before he dies?'

'I'd say it's poppycock. I've kept in contact with Miss Craig since the murder and if anything, her desire to see Clairmont face justice has grown stronger over the years. If she had any idea where he was she would have informed the police immediately.'

'So why *do* you think she's returned to Saxted after all this time?'

'I'm afraid I have no idea. It's just one more mystery to add to the baffling events surrounding this case.'

'Keith Treadwell, thank you very much.' The reporter turned to the camera. 'So the mystery continues and if you want to know more about the murder at Elysium you can find a link to Keith Treadwell's website on our webpages.'

I gave back the laptop, whistled to Oz and headed for the door.

Bailey looked up. 'Get yourself a new phone.'

'Can't. I'm skint.'

'You should sell your story – *Meals on wheels boy tells all! My secret chats with tragic Norma.*'

'Yeah . . . funny.'

He stopped smiling. 'I'm not kidding about the phone. You don't want to go walking into trouble without one.'

'I'll have to risk it.'

He groaned, heaved himself up and pointed to the couch. 'Tip it up.'

I turned the couch up and squatted down, not sure what I was supposed to be looking at till he tugged back the thick black covering and took out the Tesco's bag stuffed between the springs. I looked inside. There must have been at least ten handsets in there, all with their chargers wrapped round them. In Jackson's line of work you could see how a stash of emergency phones might come in handy.

'Pick one. They're all charged up with money on the SIM.'

Voices sounded on the walkway, followed by the rattle of keys. I stuffed the nearest phone into my backpack and tipped the couch back. Bailey threw himself across the cushions, reached for the remote and turned the TV up loud.

'Not a word,' he croaked as footsteps thudded down the hall.

Was he kidding? I was desperate, not suicidal.

CHAPTER 13

I felt bad leaving Bailey on his own but he seemed all right stretched out in his favourite spot by the window, with Treadwell's website on his screen and his bird's-eye view of the estate. While he was off school there wouldn't be much happening on Farm Street that he didn't know about.

I got the tube to Shepherd's Bush and walked down Goldhawk Road, keeping a constant watch for anyone following me. Oz was wary too, staying close, keeping his head down and his ears pricked.

The Besedka was a big glass-fronted restaurant with its name picked out in flickery blue lights above the window. The inside was decked out with cheap plastic tables and chairs and faded photo murals of mountains and forests. It was pretty packed and there were four or five harassed waitresses scurrying around balancing trays. Trying to look like I dropped in on Ukrainian gang bosses on a regular basis I pushed through the crowded tables and asked the big guy at the till for Mr Kozek.

He laughed but you could see the joke was on me.

'Get lost, kid. And get that dog out of here.'

I scooped Oz up and tried to stop him wriggling. 'It's business. It's important.'

'I said, get lost.'

When I didn't budge he slammed the till shut and started moving round from behind the counter. Oz let out a low growl and bared his teeth. I clamped my hand over his muzzle.

'Tell him . . . tell him I'm a friend of Jackson Duval's,' I said.

I didn't have much of a plan but mentioning Jackson definitely hadn't been part of it.

The man eyeballed me for a second, then he called something to the waitress heading through the swing doors. Seconds later she came back with a hulk with a greasy black quiff, poached egg eyes and a tattooed neck. When I say big I'm talking at least six foot six, and when I say neck I mean a solid slab of muscle that sloped from the top of his arms straight to his ears. Just looking at him made me want to pee myself and run. Too late now. The Hulk had already joined in the laughter. He grabbed me by the neck and next thing I knew I was being shoved into the kitchens and hustled past rows of sweaty cooks and bubbling saucepans, spitting steam.

My bad case of jitters turned into a full-blown

freak-out when he made me put Oz down and frisked me. Did I look like I'd got an AK47 stuffed down my trousers? He even jerked Oz's head up and felt under is collar, raising a big menacing hand when Oz snapped at him.

'Stop it Oz, It's OK,' I said quickly.

Once the Hulk had satisfied himself that neither of us was armed he took me upstairs, knocked at a door and shouted something I couldn't understand. I heard a click and a whir. The door swung open. Viktor Kozek obviously didn't like visitors barging in unexpectedly.

The Hulk pushed me into a plush-looking office with a red carpet, wood panelling and no windows. Above the desk hung a big wall-mounted screen, chequered with grainy, ever-changing CCTV shots of a warehouse, a garage forecourt, a bar and a row of railway arches. The man sitting at the desk was about fifty. His pudgy cheeks, short grey-flecked hair and natty pinstriped suit made him look like everybody's favourite uncle till you saw his eyes, which were very blue, very scary and very busy taking in every detail of my face.

'Who are you?' he said. His voice was low and suspicious and his accent was similar to Yuri's.

I swallowed down the sick taste of panic and said the first name that popped into my head. 'Erm, Erroll Potts.'

He pointed to a flashy red velvet chair. Oz was agitated, letting out grunty little whines. He wanted to leave. Me too. I sat down and pushed him onto the floor next to me.

'Lie still. Keep quiet.' I hissed.

He dropped his nose on his paws and cowered there glancing warily from side to side.

'Did Jackson Duval send you?'

'Not . . . exactly, Mr Kozek.'

Viktor's frown got deeper. 'What do you want?'

I opened my mouth. Nothing came out. Then I remembered I was doing this for Mum and my tongue loosened up.

'I'm looking for someone,' I said. 'A Ukrainian called Yuri. I don't know his second name but he's been in the UK a couple of weeks and I think he's in London.'

'What makes you think I can help you?'

'He's in trouble. I think he's involved in some . . . stuff.'

'What sort of stuff?'

'Bad stuff. He's on the run.'

He rocked forward slightly in his chair. 'Who from?'

'I don't know.'

'Why do you want him?'

'He's . . . got something I need.' I wasn't going to tell Viktor it was information.

'Something valuable?'

'Only to me,' I said, quickly. 'So if you know anyone who could do some quiet asking around I can pay with this.' I pulled out the tie-clip.

He took it, curling his lip.

'What is this?'

'It's gold and that's a real diamond.'

He sucked his teeth and tossed it back to me. 'Second-hand diamonds aren't my line. But I have to admit, you intrigue me, Erroll. I was about to have some Russian tea. Will you join me?'

'Erm . . . OK,' I said, hating the wobble in my voice.

'Bogdan!' He shouted something to the Hulk, who grunted and lumbered off. Then he got out a little digital recorder, pressed a couple of buttons and laid it on the desk between us.

'Nothing personal, Erroll. Whenever I have an interesting conversation with someone I don't know l always find it pays to take a few precautions.' He settled back in his leather chair, 'So, What does this Yuri look like?'

I took a deep breath and started to describe him. I'd just got to the gash on his leg when Bogdan shouted to be buzzed in. He came back followed by a girl carrying two steaming glasses of black tea in silver holders on a fancy silver tray. She was maybe a bit older than me, pale, skinny and not very tall, with a slightly crooked mouth and long, dead straight hair that was this weird silvery colour. I guessed she was Viktor's daughter, till I noticed she wasn't dressed like a rich man's kid and saw the look he gave her, which wasn't exactly bursting with fatherly affection. She had a right sour face on her, didn't smile or even look up. She served Viktor first. Then she turned, and as she got to me she glimpsed Oz's head poking round the other side of my chair, missed her footing and slopped boiling tea all down my hand and on to the carpet.

Three things happened. I let out a yelp. Viktor bawled Nina! and the girl looked me in the eye. She wasn't sour. She was terrified.

'Hey, my fault,' I said, wincing with pain. 'Sorry about your carpet, Mr Kozek. I've . . . always been clumsy.'

Viktor snapped something at the girl. She scooted away and came back with a cloth, a bowl of water and a little dish of ice. As I held a lump of it against my hand she mouthed me a silent *thank you*, rolled up her sleeves and started scrubbing at the stain. It was then that I saw the purple bruises. Rings of them like bracelets. As if someone with powerful fingers had grabbed her wrists and squeezed very hard.

'Does this Yuri have tattoos?' Viktor said.

'Yeah,' I said, tearing my eyes away from the girl's arms. 'All over.'

'Describe them.'

He sat forward, nodding slightly when I told him about the spiders and the snarling wolf on Yuri's back, and pressing me for numbers when I mentioned the domed turrets.

'What's it matter how many?'

'They are jail tattoos. One dome, one year in prison.'

I shuddered. There'd been twelve, maybe fifteen turrets, rippling between Yuri's shoulder blades.

'What do the others mean?'

He shrugged. 'Every prison, every gang, they have their own variations. But if you know how to read them they can tell you a man's whole life story.'

I glanced at the little tattooed snake peeking out from under his cuff, and looked away as he adjusted his sleeve.

'What tattoos does he have on his chest?' Viktor said.

For all he was trying to look bored, something shifted when I told him about the one-eyed skull and the barbed wire. When I asked him what it meant he shrugged again but his whole body was tense.

'Where did you last see him?'

A warning light flashed in my head. 'Er . . . Brixton. He was just passing through. Not sure where he was headed.'

'He speak English?'

'Yes. It's a bit rusty but he understands everything.'

'So you think he's been to UK before?'

'Maybe.'

'And you are hoping he has made contact with old friends.'

'Yeah.'

Viktor switched off his tape recorder.

'Erroll, I have enjoyed our little chat and as a favour to Jackson Duval I will ask my people to keep an eye out for this Yuri. But it is very hard to find a man who does not want to be found, especially in a place like London.'

Nina had been so quiet I'd almost forgotten she was there till she picked up her bowl and cloth and backed out the door.

'OK,' I said, ' but . . . if it's all right with you can we keep Jackson out of this? He thought I . . . shouldn't get involved.'

'You can trust me, Erroll.'

His smile was slow, lingered just a little too long, and brought back the panic.

'Bogdan will show you out.'

I didn't mention that he hadn't asked for my number. What was the point? We both knew he was never going to call.

Oz skulked along at my heels, keeping well clear of the Hulk. The kitchen was even steamier and nosier than before, full of shouting people blocking the narrow space between the counters. I swerved to avoid a waitress, nearly braining myself on a row of dangling saucepans.

Nina cut past me, lugging a tray piled high with dirty plates. I nodded at her. She didn't nod back, just gave me this strange look, like she was sussing me out. Then she blinked down at the tray and back up at me. I thought she'd got something in her eye. She did it again.

I followed her gaze. A tiny strip of paper was poking out from under the plates, all curled up like a little white worm.

She stared at me, willing me to pick it up. I palmed it and kept walking through the swing doors, speeding up as I followed Bogdan across the restaurant. By the time I hit the street I was running. I didn't stop till I was well clear of the Besedka and everybody in it. I darted down an alley and stood with my back to the wall breathing fast, trying to imagine the story that the one-eyed skull on Yuri's chest was telling. Kozek knew what it was, that was for sure. But the rings of bruises on Nina's scrawny arm kept blotting out Yuri's tattoos, hinting at a pretty miserable tale of their own.

I flattened out the strip of paper. She hadn't taken any chances. The pencilled letters were so faint you had to know you were looking for something to even see they were there.

Tonight 10 p.m. Tina's burger van. Shepherd's Bush Market.

Half of me wanted to chuck it in the nearest bin and keep running; the other half was desperate to know what she wanted. I was so confused I called Bailey and told him

129

about my meeting with Viktor. He went ballistic when I admitted I'd mentioned Jackson. Who could blame him? I kept telling him it was OK because Viktor wasn't going to help me anyway and when he finally calmed down I told him about Nina.

'What's she playing at?' he said.

'She's got bruises, all round her wrists.'

'Doesn't mean you can trust her.'

'I bet it was that creep Kozek who gave them to her. She wouldn't risk upsetting him unless it was really important.'

'Or he put her up to it.'

'Either way, I've got to find out what she wants.'

'Maybe she fancies you.'

'What? No. She's not like that. She's . . . I dunno, kind of angry.'

I hung up, bought some chips and joined the rest of the homeless hanging out on Shepherd's Bush Green. Most of them had scraggy dogs and looked like life had given them a good kicking. Me and Oz fitted right in.

After an hour or so of trying to figure out why Nina wanted to see me, why Viktor Kozek had got so uptight about Yuri's skull tattoo, and what Jackson would do to me and Bailey if he found out where I'd been, my brain was hitting overload. But I didn't want to stop. Whenever I did, the thought of Mum reaching out to that fireman rushed in to fill the gap and the name Lizzie echoed round my head, pitching me into a bottomless blur of pain. The only way to stop falling was to keep going.

*

I didn't like it. I didn't like the broken street lamps, the boarded-up railway arches or the unfamiliar tags on the walls. Most of all I didn't like the groups of kids hanging round the entrance to the market looking for trouble. I put Oz on the lead and slipped down a shadowy alleyway that led into the main part of the market. It was deserted, lit only by a few yellowish street lamps, and everything was locked up, chained up or battened down. I kept walking between the rows of empty stalls, listening to the tarpaulins flapping in the wind and searching for Tina's burger van.

When I found it, it was nothing special, just a dirty old caravan with a scabby-looking burger and a couple of hot dogs painted on the closed metal shutters. Nina wasn't there. I hung around for a couple of minutes watching for movement in the shadows, jumping every time Oz's ears pricked up or the wind rattled an awning till I got so freaked out I backed between a couple of skips and called Bailey.

'What's happening?' he said.

'Nothing. She's not here.'

'Get out of there, it might be a trap.'

'I'll give it five minutes then I'll . . .'

'Hey, Erroll.' It was a thin, sharp girl's voice that made Erroll sound like earhole. Didn't bother me, it wasn't my name.

I leant out and took a look down the line of stalls.

The girl's voice came again. 'Can anyone see you?'

'No.'

'Down here.'

'Watch yourself,' Bailey said.

The tarpaulin round the bottom of the nearest stall opened like a curtain. A hand poked out, beckoning me inside. Suddenly I wasn't so sure this was a good idea. I thumbed the 'end call' button but didn't press it. I mean, if this *was* a set-up, having Bailey listening in would be some kind of backup. And like Viktor Kozek said, if you're having a meeting with a stranger, it pays to take a few precautions. I hissed 'shh' into the phone, hoping Bailey would get what I was doing, and slipped the handset into the front pocket of my jeans.

I scrambled through the flapping tarpaulin and pulled Oz in after me. Even with our knees bunched up there was barely room for her and me, let alone a dog as well. But Nina didn't seem to mind and neither did Oz. He climbed between us, wriggling his head under her arm and thumping his tail against my face.

'This is cosy,' I said.

She flicked on a little torch that gave off a dim yellow light but even then I couldn't see much of her face. She'd got an old woolly hat pulled over her eyes and a dark scarf wrapped round her mouth. She pulled it forward just enough to speak. 'I have not much time. Why are you looking for this man called Yuri?' She said her Ws like Vs just like Yuri and Viktor.

'He's in trouble. I want to help him.'

Her pinched little face was wary. 'That is all?'

'No. I think he knows something . . . 'bout my mum.'

She shifted round to give Oz more room. 'Like what?'

'Like why she died.'

It weirded me out the way she just nodded as if she had conversations like this all the time.

'I can help you find him,' she said.

'What's in it for you?'

'Cash.'

'Why do you need it?'

'My father owes Viktor money.'

'How much?'

'A lot.'

'I don't have any. Not right now.' I pulled out the tie-clip. 'But I'm going to try and sell this.'

She plucked it out of my fingers, turning it so it sparkled in the torch light. 'What is this?'

'A tie-clip.'

She handed it back. 'If it is stolen maybe you will not get much. What about Yuri? Can he get me money?'

I thought about the emeralds in his Oxo tin and said, 'Yeah, maybe.'

'OK. I will take tie-clip as down payment.'

'On what?'

'Information.'

'It better be worth it.'

She leant back and put a hand up to stop Oz licking her face. 'How about this? After you left, Viktor called his brothers in Ukraine. They are big criminals, just like him. They made some calls and now Viktor is pretty sure who Yuri is.'

My heart did a double beat. 'How come?'

'He has prison tattoos. They make it easy.'

I stared at her, suddenly suspicious. 'How do you know who Viktor talked to?'

She dropped her eyes. 'I hear things.'

'How?'

'I listen.'

'So why did Viktor say he couldn't help me?'

'Do we have deal?'

I nodded and held out the tie-clip. 'Go on. Why did he lie?'

She didn't take it. 'First I must know if I can trust you. Who told you about Viktor?'

'My mate Bailey. He said his brother Jackson did business with him.'

Her eyes widened. 'Jackson Duval?'

'Yeah.'

'Swear to me you will not tell Jackson I am helping you.'

'I swear. In any case, he'll string me up if he finds out I've been anywhere near Viktor Kozek.'

She turned this over for a minute then said. 'OK. So now I need all details – how you know Yuri and how he knows about your mother.'

For the third time that day I outlined the weird links between Lincoln, Mum and Yuri. I even told her about Yuri hiding at Elysium, and my nan working for Norma Craig and Greville Clairmont before the murder. If it was a test it looked like I passed because as soon as I'd finished she pocketed the tie-clip.

'OK. Well, you are not only one who is looking for Yuri,' she said. 'Viktor is going to find him and sell him to someone who will give him a lot of money.'

Sell him! I felt like someone had punched me. 'Who . . .

134

who wants to buy him?' I could hardly force out the words.

'A Russian Mafia boss.'

'What's he called?'

'No one knows his real name and no one gets to see him. But they call him *Korshun*.' She frowned. 'It means something like . . . um . . . Vulture.'

'Some nickname. How much is he offering?'

'Half a million pounds.'

'For Yuri?' I was stunned. 'Why so much?'

'Viktor's brothers do not know. But they say his name is Yuri Borzov and till few weeks ago he was in Strizhavka Jail.'

'Strizhavka?'

The word pinballed round my brain a couple of times and hit a memory. Lincoln's insurance form. The first document I'd opened on his laptop.

Name: Ivo Horatio Lincoln
Place of theft: Oselya Guest House, Strizhavka, Ukraine
Items stolen: Apple Mac laptop, Samsung camera, leather bag, books

'You're sure it was Strizhavka?'

'Of course.' Her voice turned bitter. 'Kozek brothers have eyes and ears in all prisons in Ukraine. Why? You know this place?'

'Ivo Lincoln was staying in Strizhavka just before he left Ukraine. And when he was there someone stole his laptop.'

She frowned at me. 'Was he visiting Yuri?'

'Maybe. I don't know. How did Yuri escape from jail?'

'Vulture's people got fake papers and took him.'

'How did they swing that?'

'Money. It can buy most things. 'Specially in Ukraine.'

'How'd he get away from the Vulture's people?'

'He attacked driver, car crashed and he escaped.'

I shot her a look. That was exactly how Yuri had told it. Any lingering suspicions I'd had about Nina or her story were fading fast.

'Since that day, Vulture's people look for him all over Ukraine,' she said. 'They have no idea where he is until today when you told Viktor he is in England.'

I smashed my fist against the rickety framework of the stall. What had I done? If I hadn't gone to Viktor, Yuri would have been all right. And now, thanks to me, he'd got no chance. It was all my fault.

'Stop!' she hissed. 'Someone will hear you. I must go. Give me your phone.'

'What?'

'I will need it.'

'Oh. Right.'

Wrestling with Oz's scrabbling legs and flapping tail, I got out the phone, and while he was trying to scramble on to Nina's lap I fumbled to cut the connection to Bailey. I shoved it into her hand. 'I'm staying with Bailey on the Farm Street. Estate. His number's in the contacts.' I squeezed my fingers into my backpack. 'Here, take the charger.'

She took it, lifted Oz off her legs and parted the

tarpaulin. I grabbed her wrist. She flinched. I remembered her bruises and let go.

'Sorry . . . I didn't mean . . .'

'What? I must hurry.'

I screwed up my eyes, trying to remember the sounds Yuri had shouted in his sleep. '*Tee gneed-a-pag-a-na-ya, Ya-za-moo-cho tebya* . . . what does it mean?'

She pulled a face. 'Why do you ask me this? It means, you filthy . . . scum. I will kill you.'

'There's something else. 'My name's not Erroll Potts. It's Joe Slattery.'

'I do not care what you are called. Just tell no one about me.'

She sprinted into the darkness. I hunkered down in that cramped little hideaway, feeling like I'd been thrown off a torpedoed ship and left clinging to a scrap of burning wreckage.

CHAPTER 14

Bailey was hunched over his laptop when I walked in. He looked up. 'You OK?'

''Course I'm not. Didn't you hear what she said about the Vulture? Every time I think about giving Yuri away to that creep Kozek I want to throw up.'

'Yeah. I heard everything Nina said. And it's got to be the lead you've been looking for. Think about it. A Mafia boss who's got a beef with Yuri is gonna have a pretty solid motive for silencing a journalist who's been nosing into Yuri's business.'

I slumped down in the armchair. 'Yeah, but what was his problem with Mum?'

'That's what we're gonna find out.'

'Then he'll kill us, too.' I looked at Bailey stuck on that couch with his tablets and inhaler lined up next him. If some crazy gangster burst in when he was on his own he wouldn't stand a chance.

'You've got to back out, Bailey. It's too dangerous.'

He snorted. 'Once Jackson gets a whiff of where you've been, we'll both be dead anyway.'

If that was his way of cheering me up it wasn't working.

'So you agree Nina's on the level?'

He pulled a face. 'Dunno. You'd have to be desperate or crazy to double-cross Viktor Kozek.'

I wandered out into the kitchen, fetched a couple of Cokes and tossed him one. 'I need another phone.'

Bailey groaned. 'What do you think I am, Phones-R-Us?'

But he stood up anyway and let me help myself from the stash under the couch.

'Once this is over I'll put it back, Jackson won't even notice,' I said.

'Yeah right. Just like you did with the last one.'

I turned on the phone, flinched when I saw Jackson's name in the contacts, and punched in Bailey and Nina's numbers.

Bailey was back on his laptop, scanning the screen. 'I've been going over what Shauna told you. She said Lincoln gave Sadie something and she thought she put it in her bag. Right?'

I nodded.

'So where is it?'

'Not in her bag. I checked already.'

'Check it again.'

I fetched Mum's bag from the carrier I'd left in Bailey's room, and tipped her things on to the floor. 'Told you, there's nothing here,' I said. 'Not unless Lincoln gave her a load of make-up, or a slushy romance.'

Oz came scampering over and started pawing Mum's stuff. I pushed him away. 'Get off. What's the matter with you?'

He wagged his tail, letting out excited little yaps. Then it hit me. He could smell Mum, too. He thought she was around somewhere, just out of sight. If she had been I bet she'd have been rolling her eyes and folding her arms, telling me I was missing something really obvious, like she did when she was watching one of her cop shows. I re-checked the pockets of her bag and went through her things again, opening all the tubes and bottles and laying them out in a row. The glittery cover of Love Me Do glinted as I snatched it up. I shook it open. A folded square of paper fluttered to the floor.

I was sure my whole body had stopped working till I saw my hands reach for the paper. I sat down next to Bailey and slowly unfolded it. It was a printout of a low-res photo, taken on a cheap camera or maybe a phone. But the image was clear enough: a sheet of lined, brownish paper with two black and white snapshots fastened to it with rusty staples.

The first one was a picture from way back of Norma Craig, looking very young in a white lacy mini-dress and gazing up at Greville Clairmont. He wasn't that much taller than her and he had a thin face, dark hair curling on to his collar and the kind of smile you don't expect a murderer to have. The second was a shot of a bit of neatly mowed lawn going down to a big fancy greenhouse full of plants. Just behind the greenhouse was a flower bed with an ivy-covered statue in the middle of it.

Bailey frowned. 'OK, so that's Norma and Clairmont – but what's with the greenhouse?'

My thoughts were churning. 'It's the one in the garden at Elysium. I recognise that statue. And you see the little door in the wall just behind it? That's the door Yuri had the key to.'

I peered closer at the picture of Clairmont. He was wearing the diamond tie-clip I'd just given to Nina. That was a shock. But it wasn't the tie-clip that was stopping me breathing. It was the number written along the top of the photo doing that. It took me a couple of seconds to find the list of numbers that I'd jotted down from Ivo's notebook and compare the two. But I already knew what I'd find. My hands shook and I struggled to keep my voice steady as I showed it to Bailey.

'This is a page from one of the files Lincoln found in the KGB archive. See, the numbers match. He must have taken this shot of it on his phone while he was in the archive.'

Bailey tapped the picture of Norma and Clairmont, took a swig of Coke and said very quietly, 'You ever wondered what really happened to Clairmont?'

''Course but—'

'Suppose he was working for the KGB. Suppose he ran off to Russia after the murder and ended up as a crime boss . . .'

I could feel this weird sensation. It was blood draining out of my face. 'You think Clairmont's the Vulture?'

He shrugged. 'Just sayin'.'

We spent most of that night picking over Bailey's theory. OK, so it sort of explained what the KGB had been doing with a photo of Norma and Clairmont but without the rest of the file we still didn't have a clue why Lincoln had come haring back to England to tell Mum about it. I mean, according to Doreen, Mum hadn't even been born when Clairmont disappeared, so it wasn't like she'd ever met him. The only thing I could think of was that for some reason my nan's name had been in the file. Maybe some Russian bigwig had visited Elysium and she'd mixed him one of her famous Martinis. But another search of her scrapbook scored a big fat zero on that front.

In the end Bailey messaged Treadwell's website, asking if he'd ever come across any hint of a KGB connection to Clairmont. Then we looked up loads of stuff about Brits spying for the Soviets back in the 60s and 70s. You'd be amazed how many toffs had been at it.

We'd stayed up talking till nearly four in the morning and I couldn't believe it when Bailey's ringtone woke us up again just before six. He thumped his hand around in the dark and switched it off. Ten seconds later it rang again. This time he answered it, talking in a thick, groggy voice like his mouth was stuffed with socks.

'Yeah . . . Yeah . . . how did you . . . What?' He sprang out of bed. 'OK. Keep your hair on. We're coming.'

He yanked the pillow off my head. 'Get up. That Nina girl's downstairs going mental.'

We scrambled into the hall, tiptoeing past Jackson's room and cringing when the front door clicked. Oz had followed us out and started tucking into a half eaten burger and chips he found on the walkway. I left him there and kept running till I spotted Nina crouched behind the wheelie bins near the bottom of the stairs, her hair stuffed into that beanie hat, and her scarf wrapped round her mouth. The minute I reached her she shoved the phone and tie-clip in my face.

'Take them,' she hissed. 'And never come near me again.'

I've never seen anyone so angry. That included Doreen.

'What have I done?'

'I told you. If Viktor finds out I help you, my whole family will be dead or worse. But you do not care. You are stupid. You have no idea what you are doing or who you are fighting. But you let your friend listen to everything I said.'

I shifted around, wondering how she'd guessed and whether it'd be worth trying to bluff it out.

'Do not think about denying this! I checked the phone. You ring this Bailey from 9.55 to 10.32 last night. This is exact time you are with me.'

Grovelling isn't pretty but when you're truly busted, believe me, it's the only option.

'Look,' I said, 'I'm really sorry, I . . . I was scared, I didn't know if I could trust you. I swear Bailey won't tell anybody anything. He's just helping me find out who killed Mum.'

If I hadn't been standing there bleary-eyed and barefoot, in a washed-out I'm with stupid T-shirt, and track pants two sizes too small, I might have stood a chance of talking her round. As it was she just got angrier.

'It is bad that you do this but worse that you are such big idiot you get caught. When you are fighting Viktor Kozek you cannot be stupid.'

That's when Bailey came wheezing down the stairs and stuck his oar in.

'Yeah, Joe's a jerk, he can't help it.'

That really helped and in his vest and baggy boxers he wasn't looking that impressive either.

'Thanks a lot,' I said.

He ignored me and took a puff on his inhaler. 'Look, I know he screwed up, but you need money and we need help so maybe we can work this out.'

She stared from him to me. Her anger had gone off the boil but it was still steaming. 'If leaving your phone on is your idea of secret bugging, you will need all help you can get.'

Bailey flicked me a glance, obviously more hopeful than I was that things were going our way. Oz came haring out of nowhere and bounded up to her.

'How did he get those scars?' she said, like she was accusing me of being a dog beater as well as a moron.

'Fighting an Alsatian.'

That did impress her. She patted his head. 'He is very brave.'

'No, very stupid. He has no idea what he's doing or who he's fighting.'

I could have sworn her lips twitched but it wasn't easy to tell if she was smiling or scowling.

'So, can we give it another go?' Bailey said.

She shoved a bit of hair back in her hat and frowned. 'Do you swear not to tell *anyone* I help you?'

We nodded.

'And when we find Yuri you make him pay me as much money as he can.'

'OK.'

I could see Bailey watching her, trying to suss her out. 'Is Viktor hassling your dad to pay off his loan?' he said.

'No,' she said, grimly. 'Not now.'

'So why are you so hung up about money?'

'I have to stop Viktor destroying him.'

'I don't get it,' Bailey said.

She sagged against the wall. 'Back in Kiev Viktor lent my father lot of money to set up security company. Company was not successful. Viktor made us come to UK to pay off debt.'

'OK.'

'No, it is not OK. Viktor makes him do terrible things.'

'Like what?'

She dropped her eyes. 'Today he is disconnecting alarms in big warehouse so that Viktor can send people to steal everything stored in there.'

'What about you?'

'At first me and my mother worked on farm. I did not mind this too much. Sometimes I even drive tractors. But now we live over garage at back of Besedka. We have one small room that is damp and dark.' Her face scrunched up.

'Sometimes Viktor makes me help my father do these bad things and sometimes he makes me clean kitchens and office at Besedka.'

'What about your mum?'

'She works in kitchen also. She is very unhappy. Viktor does not care. He thinks he owns us and we cannot get away.'

'Can't you go back to Ukraine?'

'We have no passports and no money. But even if we get home how can we hide from Viktor's brothers? No. We must buy our freedom. I must go now. I start to work at eight.' I held out the phone and tie-clip. She nodded and took them. 'Remember, both of you, tell no one that I help you find Yuri. Viktor Kozek is very bad man but compare him to Vulture and he is saint.'

Although Jackson was a late riser and a heavy sleeper, Rikki wasn't and we got back to the flat to find Danielle shuffling round the kitchen in her dressing gown, warming his bottle and demanding to know where we'd been. But as soon as Bailey offered to feed him she shut up and went back to bed, which was kind of the plan. Then he dumped me with Rikki and went straight back to his laptop. I'd never have kept a two-year-old quiet for ten seconds without Oz, who turned out to be surprisingly cool about having his tail pulled and his eyes poked. But even he drew the line at getting whacked round the head with a rubber giraffe. Bailey kept up a running commentary the whole time on the stuff he was looking at. He was showing me an old newspaper article about the Clairmont emeralds and getting me to confirm that they were definitely the ones in Yuri's Oxo tin when a message pinged into his inbox. You'd have thought he'd won the lottery when he realised it was from Treadwell. He read it out over Rikki's babbling.

Dear Bailey,

Thanks for your inquiry. It's good to know that a new generation is taking an interest in this old but continually mystifying case. Given the political climate of the 1960s and 70s I did consider the possibility that Clairmont had been spying for the Russian KGB and escaped from the UK with their help. However, no evidence has ever come to light to support this theory. That said, so many powerful people visited Elysium at one time or another it would have been a perfect cover for such activity and in the murky world of Cold War espionage no theory, however far-fetched, can ever be discounted. Please let me know if you come across any evidence you think might be relevant to the investigation. I once made a pledge to see this case solved before I die and time is ticking on!

Keith Treadwell

Bailey carefully filed the email. 'Like he says, Elysium would have been a great place for spies to hang out. All those ministers and army types getting drunk and spilling their secrets.' His face lit up. 'Yeah. How about this for a theory? Norma found out Clairmont was running a spy ring and that's why he tried to murder her!'

I turned and stared at him, trying the idea out, seeing if

it held up against everything we knew. The more I thought about it, the more questions it started to answer.

'That could be what Ivo Lincoln discovered in the KGB archive.' I said, slowly

He stared down at his laptop. The screen was reflected in his glasses as if his eyes were connecting directly to the drives.

'And maybe your nan caught Clairmont doing something dodgy without realising exactly what he was up to. So he sent the KGB a report about it, just in case she worked it out.' Bailey grinned, dead pleased with himself, and for a second I felt this soaring rush of excitement. Then it stalled and crashed.

'It's all just theories,' I said. 'If we're going to prove any of it we've still got to find out exactly what Lincoln discovered in those KGB files and then we've got to find Yuri.'

I got out the envelope that Yuri had sent me the tie-clip in and rechecked the smudged postmark.

'You got a magnifying glass,' I said, snatching Bailey's inhaler away from Rikki.

All Bailey could come up with was a glass paperweight that his mum had won in a church tombola. It wasn't easy seeing round the purple plastic flower in the middle and even when I managed to find a clear bit of glass it made everything go squiffy. But it was better than nothing. I laid it over the postmark, tilting and rolling the glass. The curve of fuzzy letters at the top started with a C or a G and almost definitely ended with a D and the blobs round the bottom were maybe SE or SW and then a 5 or it could have been a 6 or an 8.

Bailey got straight on to it and started checking out all the South London post codes for districts starting with C or G. SW6 was Fulham, so that wasn't it. SE5 covered Denmark Hill, Peckham and *Camberwell* which got us excited for a bit but it was too long and didn't end with a D. SW5 was Earls Court, SE6 was places I'd never heard of – Bellingham, Hither Green and *Catford*. I watched the smudges swim beneath the glass, beginning to doubt what I was seeing.

'That's got to be right. It's the only possible match.' I said.

'So now we know he posted a tie-clip in Catford a week ago.' Bailey said. 'It's not much to go on.'

'It's one step ahead of Viktor Kozek,' I said.

The Professor was due back from the Edinburgh and all that day I kept phoning and texting him, desperate to know if the copies of the files had arrived from the archive. He was always on voice mail and it was gone ten that night when his name flashed up on my phone.

'Hey, Professor,' I said. 'Any news?'

'That's why I'm calling. I just got back to find a package from Kiev.'

His attempt to sound breezy wasn't working, and as for me, my mouth had gone so dry I could hardly speak. 'What's in it?'

'I don't know.' The breeziness disappeared and his voice sank to a croak 'When it came to opening it, I just couldn't do it. Not on my own. I couldn't face what I might find. I thought . . . well, I thought we could open it together. Could you scrape together the fare and come over tomorrow? I'll reimburse you the minute you get here.'

'Yeah, I'll borrow some money off a mate. I'll get the first train.'

'Fine. I'm an early riser, and anyway, I don't think I'll be getting much sleep.'

We'll open the package, then we'll take the files round to a Russian-speaking colleague of mine. I'm sure he'll give us the gist of what's in them.'

'I've got some news I'll tell you tomorrow but while you're there can you remember Ivo ever mentioning anyone called Lizzie?'

He thought for a minute. 'Not off the top of my head. Sorry.'

'No worries. I'll see you tomorrow.'

The Professor wasn't the only one who had trouble sleeping that night. By five next morning I was on the train to Cambridge, watching the sky lighten over London and imagining my fingers ripping open that package and finding out who had ordered Mum's death.

CHAPTER 15

Bailey had given me every penny he had – thirty quid – so I splashed out on a cab from the station and sprinted to St Saviour's. The main gates were still locked so I went into the porters' lodge. Albert Brewster, the head porter, peered over his mug of tea, recognised me and nodded. 'You're up early.'

'I'm having breakfast with Professor Lincoln.'

'So he told me.' He threw a glance at Oz. 'Make sure that dog behaves himself. Can you remember the way?'

'Yes, thanks.'

He waved me into the misty quiet of the courtyard. All the windows were dark and the only sounds were my footsteps and Oz's raspy breath as we pounded across the flagstones and swerved through the deserted corridors and covered walkways. Speeding round a corner I nearly ploughed into a bunch of burly blokes in singlets getting marched towards the river by a bossy-looking girl, about half their size, with 'Cox' written on her cap. This place was truly weird.

I dodged past them and raced towards the Professor's staircase. The little wooden in/out sign at the bottom of the stairs was flicked to out. I took no notice, guessing he'd been tired when he got back and forgotten to change it. Bounding upstairs, I took the last half-dozen steps in one leap and pulled up short on the landing, surprised by the 'Do Not Disturb' sign hanging on his door.

There was an old wooden bench under the window and I'd just sat down on it, wondering what to do, when I heard raised voices from inside. I jumped up and rapped hard on the door. Instead of a cheery call to come in, or the sound of locks and doorknobs turning, the shouting just carried on, as if whoever was doing it hadn't even noticed the knocking. Reckoning the Professor had the radio on too loud to hear me I pressed my ear to the panelling. Close up the voices didn't sound much like they were coming from the breakfast news, not unless they were doing a report on grunting and stomping around.

The skin down my spine felt suddenly tighter. I tried the handle. It was locked from the inside and wouldn't budge. I tied Oz to the bench, edged back down the stairs, and ran through a stone archway and on to the bridge across the river, hoping to get a glimpse into the Professor's rooms from the opposite bank. They windows were too high up. All I could see was a gleam of light flickering through the diamond-shaped panes. I started checking for another way in. There were just five arched windows in the whole of that long stone wall – one smallish one that belonged to the landing outside the Prof's door, then a space with a rusty drainpipe running down the middle of it, followed by the three big windows that belonged to the Prof's sitting room. Underneath them was a sheer drop of about twenty feet going straight into the river. Above them was a steep sloping roof.

A shadowy movement in the Professor's room got me imagining all sorts but I'd look a right idiot if I got the porter to unlock the door and we burst in on him with a personal trainer or worse still a *girlfriend*. Neither seemed very likely but I've been wrong before. I headed back, all ready to knock again and I'd just reached the top of the stairs when a crash shook the door, shattering any doubt that the Professor was in trouble. Pulling off my rucksack I jumped over Oz, climbed on to the bench, yanked open the window and hoisted myself on to the sill. Oz tried to scrabble up after me.

'Shh, get down,' I whispered. 'I'm just going to take a look.'

I shoved my top half through the gap, swung my right leg out, leant over, grabbed the drainpipe with my right hand and, by practically doing the splits managed to keep my left knee hooked over the windowsill while I pressed my right foot against one of the brackets holding up the drainpipe. Trying to ignore the twenty-foot drop, the murky, fast-flowing water and the agony in my legs. I got both hands round the pipe and craned my neck back as far as I could. But there was still no way I could see into the

Professor's room, let alone make it across the wall to his window. So there I was, splayed out like a split chicken, wondering how I was going to get back to the landing, when a cry from the Prof's room jolted my mind off my problems and back on to his. I let go with my right hand, fumbled for my phone and tried to dial 999. That was plan A, and it might have worked if there'd been a signal. But there wasn't. I went for plan B. Selecting video, I leant back, held the phone out towards the Prof's window and pressed zoom. My left arm was popping its socket and the drainpipe was definitely shifting, but I screwed up my eyes and counted to fifteen, slow as I could, before I pulled my arm back and pressed review. The blurry images playing on that little screen blanked out everything, even the pain. Two big blokes in ski masks had got the Professor tied to a chair and from the way they were punching him and shouting it looked like they were interrogating him.

'What the hell do you think you're doing?' The voice was screechy, snotty and angry.

I looked down. The burly blokes in singlets were right underneath me, packed into a row boat, sweat glistening off their muscles, with that bossy girl cox perched up one end, glaring up at me like I was the devil in trainers. Words usually come easy to me but right then I was stumped for something snappy enough to cut through the way things looked and get them on side before the Prof got killed.

'Hey, catch this.' I said and dropped the phone straight down towards the boat.

The cox's responses were pretty quick. She leant forward and snatched it out of the air.

'They've got Professor Lincoln,' I shouted. 'Play the video.'

She jabbed the buttons, squinted at the screen and without even looking up started hollering at the rowers who jumped to it without a murmur and started rowing like maniacs. I was coming round to this girl. Within seconds she'd got all eight of those massive blokes scrabbling up the side of the bridge and heading into the college.

Next thing I knew the Professor's window flew open and a meaty hand attached to a bloke in a ski mask reached out, clamped itself round my right arm and started to haul me inside. My left leg was losing hold of the windowsill and my left hand was scrabbling at the wall when I heard a shout and two more pairs of hands reached out of the landing window and grabbed my ankle. For a few excruciating minutes I hung there, stretched out like a human tug-of-war, then the sky suddenly swung away, the river hurtled towards me and my head bounced off the wall, practically knocking me out. At least it numbed the pain of my face being scraped up the stonework by the two rowers who were dragging me up to the landing and dumping me on to the floor.

Oz pawed at my bruised chest, and in a sick daze I watched the cox barking orders at the rowers. Four on each side, she'd got them lifting the bench and ramming it against the door, moving to the steady beat she was shouting. The thick slab of oak put up a tough fight but gave way in the end with a splintering thud.

I crawled forward and peered through the rowers' legs. The Professor's sitting room was in chaos. Papers everywhere, furniture kicked around, lamps smashed and in the middle of the mess, the Prof, tied to a chair, unconscious, blood spattered and alone.

I pushed through the mass of sweaty bodies and ran towards him, tearing at the ropes round his hands and shouting his name. A blur of cops, ambulance men and porters came rushing in. Someone pulled me away and I caught the flash of an oxygen mask before a ring of green uniforms blotted the Professor from view. A small window high up on the other side of the room was swinging open on its hinges. I stared out at the slope of tiles leading up to an easy escape route across the rooftops of Cambridge. Two paramedics carried the Professor off on a stretcher. Another one pushed me on to a chair and started dabbing at the cut on my forehead with some sharp-smelling stuff that stung a lot while the cops peered at the footage on my phone, talked into their radios and questioned the rowers. Then I saw it, sticking up through the mess on the desk: a large brown envelope with a foreign stamp on the front.

I couldn't take my eyes off it, not even when the cop in charge was taking my statement. What with the letter from the archive lying inches away and the bash I'd just got on the head, I was worried I'd be too fuddled to get my story straight. But it was OK. As far as the cops were concerned the Professor had been helping me deal with Mum's death and I'd saved him from ruthless burglars who were probably after his priceless coin collection. That was fine by me. No way was I telling them the real reason for my visit or my suspicions that the blokes in ski masks were working for a Russian crime boss.

My eyes swivelled back to the envelope. 'Can I go now, officer? I want to go and see how the Professor's doing.'

'Yes, but we'll need to contact you again, Joe. What's your address?'

That threw me for a minute. I gulped and gave them Doreen's.

He called out to one of the WPCs. 'Give him a lift will you, Tracey? He wants to go to the hospital.'

I'd got my move all planned out. Lifting Oz up so he hung forward and tried to wriggle free I pushed through the squash of people and as I got to the Prof's desk I let him go. In the confusion of scrabbling paws and flying paper I managed to grab the envelope and slip it under my hoodie.

'You can't take that dog in the hospital, you know.'

I looked up. It was Albert the head porter

'Don't you worry,' he said, gruffly. "You take your time. I'll find him something to eat and we'll have him in the lodge.'

'Thanks, Albert,' I said.

'Give the Prof my best.' He tutted and shook his head. 'After all he's been through. He doesn't deserve this, he really doesn't.'

The scrape and whoosh of the swing doors and the hospital smell tipped me straight back into the night

Mum died. The nightmare, siren-screaming ride in the back of the police car. Sitting with Eddy and WPC Lauren Burnett on those grey plastic waiting-room chairs. Praying for a miracle. Knowing it wasn't going to happen. Knowing Mum was beyond help by the time they got her to the operating theatre. Knowing that if Eddy didn't shut up I was going to ram my Styrofoam coffee cup right down his whingeing, whining throat.

'I've come to see Professor Lincoln.'

'Are you family?'

I could have told the truth and said, no, I've only met him three times. Instead I said 'Um . . .yes.' And it didn't feel like a lie.

The receptionist pointed me to intensive care where a short bossy nurse ordered me to sterilise my hands before grudgingly letting me through to the unit. The Professor was in a partitioned-off area, one of about six overlooked by an open-plan nurses' station. I could see a young dark-haired woman sitting beside the bed with her head in her hands. I went over to her. She looked up.

'I'm Joe Slattery,' I said.

She stumbled towards me, hair tangled, eyes floating in two sunken saucers of shock and her cardigan buttoned up the wrong way. I recognised her from the photos on the Prof's mantelpiece but only just. It was his daughter, Bitsy. She didn't say a word, just opened her arms and hugged me. I didn't even know her and I was hugging her back as if letting go would make us both disappear.

We sat down beside the bed and I looked at the Prof lying there covered in tubes, all wizened and grey like a captured alien in a sci-fi movie.

'You saved him,' Bitsy said. 'If it hadn't been for you . . . he'd be dead for sure. Why, Joe? Why would anyone do this to him?'

'No idea.'

It was another lie. Ivo requested those KGB files and he ends up dead. The Prof requested them and he ends up in intensive care. I glanced nervously through the blinds. All that was stopping the Vulture's people walking in to finish him off was a handful of nurses.

'Can we get him police protection?' I said.

'They don't do that for burglary victims.'

'Yeah, but s'posing the attackers had some other motive?'

She gave me a funny look. 'Like what?'

I shrugged. I wasn't going to tell her and put her in danger too.

A sob broke through her lips. 'No one in their right mind would want to hurt Dad.'

'He'll be all right.'

'They're not holding out much hope. It's not just the concussion, it's his heart . . . and after the shock of Ivo . . .' She rammed a soggy tissue into her eyes. 'How could they do this to him?'

I stole another look at the Prof's battered body. The guilt eating me up was tinged with terror that he'd told them everything about our investigation. Who could blame him if he had? If a couple of thugs were beating me to a pulp I'd probably tell them anything they wanted to know.

I bit back a surge of fear and fury. Fear of what the

Vulture was capable of and fury that he thought he could get away with it.

'I'll fetch us some coffee,' I said.

I left her sitting there, ran for the nearest toilet, locked myself in one of the stalls and took out the package from the archive. This was it. These documents were going to prove that Greville Clairmont was the Vulture and reveal why he'd ordered Mum's death. And now I'd got them I was going to make him pay for what he'd done to Mum, Lincoln, Yuri and now the Professor. I ripped open the envelope. Inside was a thick glossy guide to the museums of Kiev and a single sheet of paper.

Dear Professor Lincoln,

I regret to inform you that the numbered files you requested do not correspond to any material in our archive.
Please let me know if I can assist you in any other matter.

Regards
Boris Kulichenko, Curator

Liar! Did Clairmont pay you to destroy them? Did you get a big fat bonus for tipping him off that the Professor wanted copies? It felt like he had people everywhere, bribing, bullying, torturing to protect his secret. And he was on to me, I was sure of that. The creep who'd nicked Ivo's laptop and spied on me in the churchyard had to be one of his thugs. It felt like I had nowhere to run to and nowhere to hide and now I was beginning to understand what it was like to be Yuri.

*

I got a couple of coffees from the machine in the corridor, hating the familiar feel of the Styrofoam cup and took them back to Bitsy. I found her curled in the chair, all twisted and trembling, tears pouring down her face. I swung round and checked the monitor. The beeping line of green was still crawling along in slow unsteady peaks.

I put down the coffees. 'What's happened?'

'His tests came back. The doctor just told me they've got to operate . . . it's his only chance.'

'When?'

'Straight away.' Her face crumpled, dragging her lips sideways. 'There's a fifty-fifty chance he won't make it. I can't face it, Joe. The waiting, the not knowing, just sitting here helpless. I can't bear it. Not after Ivo.'

I couldn't bear it either. Not after Mum. I wanted to run out of there and get as far away from that hospital smell and those bleeping monitors as I could.

'Don't worry,' I said. 'I'll stay with you.'

CHAPTER 16

I sat with Bitsy in the waiting area, squeezed in beside the rest of the grim-faced people waiting for news from the operating suite. We didn't say much, just sat there staring helplessly at the red lino floor. After a while Bitsy dropped off into a hunched jerky sleep. I envied her. My eyes were itchy with tiredness but the one time I nodded off, the black 4x4 came screeching out of the darkness, morphed into a shrieking vulture and swooped towards me, Yuri and the Professor, getting closer and closer till the whoosh of wings, the slash of talons and a gasp of *Tell Joe and Lizzie* woke me up. Now I knew why Yuri shouted in his sleep and I was truly gutted that it was me who'd made his hunted, hellish existence a million times worse. I jumped up. There might be nothing I could do for the Professor but there was still a chance I could find Yuri before the Vulture got him.

I ran out of the hospital entrance, round the side of the main building and sat on some concrete steps going up to a fire door. The cool air stung the cut on my forehead and woke my brain up. I checked for anyone watching then I texted Nina, telling her to call me as soon as she could. I sat there for nearly twenty minutes, budging up every now and then to make room for patients in hospital gowns sneaking out for a fag.

Finally my phone beeped.

'Hey, Nina. Any news?'

'I am not sure. Vulture's people came early this morning. Then old man I have not seen before went up to office. He was English. He had list of people he called *fences*. What does this mean?'

'They buy stolen stuff then sell it.' Mum's obsession with cop shows was coming in useful.

'Yes, that makes sense. Old man said these are *fences* who have big knowledge of jewels.' My brain started to fizz. 'But list was very long, many names, many addresses, some not in London. Viktor got angry. He said there are too many. He was swearing and shouting.'

'You're sure this list was to do with finding Yuri?'

'Everything Viktor does in these days is to find Yuri. The Vulture has put money up to one million pounds. But only if he brings Yuri in by tomorrow.'

'A *millon*? Why the deadline?'

'Viktor does not know. But you think maybe Yuri has jewels he tried to sell?'

Pictures of the glittering emeralds in Yuri's Oxo tin slid

163

through my head. Glancing round I moved away from a couple of newly arrived smokers.

'Joe? Joe, are you there?' Nina hissed.

'Yeah, I'm here. And yeah, Yuri does have some jewels. Some famous emeralds.'

'What do you mean famous?'

'They're very old and worth a mint. Greville Clairmont had them with him on the day of the murder. There was stuff about them in the papers.'

I could sense her turning this over. 'How did Yuri get these emeralds?'

'I . . . I think he must have found them at Elysium,' I said, trying to ignore all the darker possibilities still hovering at the back of my brain. I walked up and down, kicking an empty fag packet around, trying to clear enough space in my head to connect the pieces. 'OK. So it looks like Yuri might have tried to sell some of the emeralds and someone recognised they were Clairmont's.'

'Yes. I think this is right.'

'Then that someone started spreading rumours round the black market. And the rumours reached the Vulture.'

'Why would Vulture think it was Yuri who tried to sell these emeralds?'

The dark possibilities started swirling around again. 'Who knows?' I said.

'Did Yuri have only emeralds?' Nina said.

'He was the one who sent me the tie-clip. He had some diamond cufflinks that matched it.'

'He *sent* you tie-clip? By postman?'

'Yeah.'

Where from?'

'Catford.'

'Cat-ford.' She said the name very slowly, drawing out the sounds. 'Are you sure?'

'Positive. It's in South London. Me and Bailey checked the postmark.' I gripped the phone hard. 'Why? What about it?'

'I think maybe I saw this Catford on Viktor's list.'

It was like catching sight of a tiny flare in a pitch-black tunnel.

'Did you see the whole address?'

'No.'

'A name?'

'No. I brought in tea. List was on desk. I saw it for maybe ten seconds.'

'Can you sneak another look at it?'

'No, Viktor and Bogdan went out and took it with them.'

'To Catford?'

'I do not think so. It was not at top of list.'

Yuri having a tin of priceless emeralds and sending post from Catford, and some well-known jewel fence living there might just be a coincidence. But it was the only lead we'd got. 'I'll go there first thing tomorrow,' I said.

'Without name or address? Where will you start?'

'I don't know.' I started pacing again. 'From what I've seen in cop shows, fences sometimes run second-hand shops or pawn-brokers as a cover. So I'll go round all the likely looking places and see if Yuri's been in. Someone might know something.'

'This is what they call *long shot*?'

'Yeah.'

'Does Catford have station?'

'S'pose.'

'I am helping my father tomorrow. I will tell him I am ill and I will meet you at Catford station at eleven o'clock.'

She didn't say what she'd be helping her father do and I didn't ask.

'Oh, and Joe there is something else.'

'What?'

'Vulture. She is woman.'

It was like she'd exploded a bomb in my head. Every theory, every clue, every bit of certainty I'd built up was cracking and crumbling.

'No. No, you're wrong. Me and Bailey worked it out. It's got to be Greville Clairmont, 'specially if he knows about the emeralds.'

'Viktor was very shocked about it, too. I am telling you. She is definitely woman.'

'Who says?'

'When Vulture's people came this morning. I brought them breakfast. I make sure I forget things, I keep coming back and I hear them talking – I must go now.'

I leant against the wall and beat the bricks till my fists were raw.

Bailey picked up on the first ring. 'Where are you? I've been trying to get you for hours,' he said.

'At the hospital. They got the Professor.'

He didn't need to ask who they were, just drew in a wheezy breath and said, 'Is he gonna be all right?'

'Dunno. They're still operating.'

'Did you get the files?'

'Nope. The curator sent a note saying they didn't exist. It's a lie. I know it is. The Vulture's people either paid him or threatened him to say it.'

'This is bad, Joe.'

'Yeah, well, I've got some more bad news. The Vulture's a woman.'

There was a long silence then all he said was, 'Interesting.'

'It's not interesting. It's a total disaster. It blows the whole KGB connection and everything else we've come up with. Now we've got nothing.'

'Maybe. Maybe not.'

That's the difference between me and Bailey, no one could ever accuse him of overreacting.

'What do you mean?'

'I've been going through your nan's scrapbook, picking out everyone who visited Elysium, and seeing what happened to them over the next few years.'

'So.'

'Out of forty names I've checked so far I've a found a German scientist who got done for spying for the Russians ten years later, a guy who got forced out of the navy because some weapons he was testing ended up in Moscow, and this business man, Ron Chapman, who'd always made a big thing about being an all American boy till it turned out he was Feliks Glazkov from some village in Siberia. So even if Clairmont wasn't running a Soviet

167

spy ring from Elysium, it looks like somebody was. And I think Ivo Lincoln found out who.'

'So why'd he go burning over to North London to tell Mum about it?'

'Search me. Maybe it was your nan.'

Even I laughed then. 'Yeah, well keep the theories coming. You might come up with something sensible.' I checked the time. 'Call you later. The Professor's coming out of surgery any minute.'

I was glad I was there when the surgeon came to find Bitsy but he talked that weird doctor-speak that could mean anything. He said the operation had gone 'as well as could be expected' but the Professor was still 'critical'. As far as I could see it just meant he wasn't dead. At least that was an improvement on the last conversation I'd had with a hospital doctor.

I spent the night in a hard plastic chair in the hospital corridor, dozing off every few minutes then waking in terror. At six Bitsy took me down to the canteen where we pretended to eat eggs and toast, and she gave me the money to get home. I felt bad taking it but she insisted. I picked Oz up from St Saviour's in a spaced-out daze of exhaustion. It was a different porter on duty. I can't say I remember his name or his face, only that he'd given Oz some left over toad in the hole for his breakfast, which was pretty decent of him. But by then the only thing I could focus on was the tiny flicker of hope that I might pick up Yuri's trail in Catford.

As soon as I got on the train I called Bailey and told

him the plan. He approved.

'I'll text you a list of pawn brokers and second-hand shops,' he said. Then he went quiet for a minute. 'Or you know what? I could bring them over, meet you there.'

'No way.'

'I'm good at detective work. You'll miss something.'

'You're sick, remember? Jackson will do his nut if you leave the flat.'

'He won't even know. Danielle's out all day and I'll be back by the time Jackson gets home.'

'S'posing something happens? I can't risk it.'

'I'm loads better today. I'll be fine.'

'You won't. You know you won't.'

'I'm going mad cooped up in here!'

'I said, no way!' I was shouting and he was shouting back.

'You can't tell me what to do!'

'Don't be an idiot. You'll get in the way!'

He started coughing, just a few croaky breaths at first then it got worse.

'I didn't mean it like that. Bailey? Are you OK? What's happening?'

I heard the squirt and suck of his inhaler.

'Shall I call Danielle?'

'I don't need a babysitter. I don't need anyone. Just butt out.'

He rang off. I'd never have shouted at him if I hadn't been so tired. I wanted to call straight back but I knew he wouldn't pick up till he'd cooled off.

I scrutinised every face in the carriage, saving them to

memory in case they were following me, then I snatched an uneasy hour of sleep. As soon as I woke up I texted Bailey. After a twenty-minute silence I texted him again and started picturing allsorts, none of it good. He'd had a relapse, the Vulture had got him. I tried calling. Got his voicemail. The panic went stratospheric when Jackson's name flashed up on the screen.

'What's happened? Is Bailey OK?'

'This ain't about Bailey.' The way he said it froze my insides.

'I'm sorry about nicking your phone, Jackson, I'll put it back.'

'This ain't about no phone. This is about Viktor Kozek. He just called me asking if I knew where you were and if you'd found Yuri. So I did some checking with Bailey and I made him tell me exactly what's been going on.'

All I managed was a couple of strangled gulps that got drowned by his stream of fury. Jackson's anger usually came out cold and sneery. Not this time. He was yelling like he'd totally lost it, sputtering and breathing funny. If I hadn't known better I'd have thought he was scared.

'I told you. You ain't up to the task of dealing with Viktor Kozek. He's into stuff I don't want nothing to do with, but your sharp little schemes are gonna bring those crazy Ukes down on all our heads. Forget about Yuri, forget about Catford and keep right outta London! You hear me?'

The phone went dead, like he'd snapped a lifeline.

I felt bad he was angry but at least if Viktor's thugs

turned up at the flat, Jackson would be looking out for Bailey. No way was I stopping the search for Yuri, though. Not now I'd come this far.

CHAPTER 17

At Catford station I did a careful check of all the passengers crowding the platform. None of the mums with screaming toddlers, grey-faced office workers or old women chewing toffees looked like they were freelancing for any Ukrainian crime bosses and no one from my carriage even left the train. So all in all, by the time Oz spotted Nina skulking behind the ticket office with her scarf pulled up and her hoodie pulled low, I'd got the queasy, hunted feeling in my stomach just about under control.

As Oz tore over to meet her, I stopped to check a text from Bailey: 'Leave Catford now!'

Yeah, right. Bailey wasn't a quitter. Jackson must have been standing over him, forcing him to send it. I didn't want to think about Jackson or what he was going to do to me for disobeying him. I shoved the phone back in my jeans.

'Hey, Nina. Do you want to get a drink or anything before we start?' I said.

'No. I need to know. Is this Yuri?'

She handed me a printout of what looked like an ID card, signed, stamped and printed in Russian. It was hard to tell if the photo was in colour because the man's staring face, his dirty uniform, the board he was holding up with a number scrawled across it and the metal bars behind him were all the same dingy shade of grey. But it was Yuri all right.

'Where'd you get it?'

'It is his prison identity card. Vulture emailed it to Viktor. I printed copy when I cleaned office.'

I didn't know what to say to that. 'Cheers' doesn't seem to cut it when someone's just risked their neck to help you.

Two kids walk into a shop and ask if any dodgy-looking Ukrainians have been in there trying to flog a load of knocked-off jewellery. It sounds like the beginning of a bad joke. Only for some reason nobody in Catford wanted to hear the punch line. You didn't need a whole lot of brain cells to see that me and Nina weren't anything to do with the law but that didn't stop us getting some pretty imaginative suggestions about what we could do with our picture of Yuri and our description of the Clairmont Emeralds.

I was going off Catford big time. Not that I'd been that enthusiastic about it to start with. Apart from some fat

173

show-off cruising past in an oversized Jeep, everyone looked skint and fed up, and the only places doing any business were the bookies and the McDonald's. The constant buzz of my phone was annoying me, too. If Jackson thought he could get Bailey to change my mind he was wrong.

We'd been traipsing around in the drizzling rain for at least an hour, trying our luck in three jewellers', two pawnshops and a couple of 'cash-for-gold' outlets when Nina stopped on the corner of a narrow side road and called me over.

'What about that place?'

It was a seedy little junk shop that called itself Fat Marty's Second-Hand Emporium. We went over to take a look. The window was crammed with heavy furniture, chipped ornaments, stained lampshades and a few bits of jewellery laid out on a table. It was mostly what Mum would have called 'old tat', except for a pear-shaped gemstone on a gold chain that was managing to sparkle even in the gloom. I watched Nina's reflection, surprised when she lost that hard-edged look and started touching her throat and tipping her head from side to side like she was imagining the necklace on. She flushed when she caught me watching her. She looked away. Her skinny shoulders stiffened.

'What's up?' I scanned the passers-by, worried she'd caught someone tailing us.

She pointed to the street sign. 'Skardu Close. I think maybe I saw something like that name on Viktor's list. It looked strange, not like English.'

A spike of adrenalin sharpened my voice. 'You got the tie-clip on you?'

'Yes.'

I glanced back at the junk shop. 'OK. We'll try something different this time. 'First we'll say we want to sell the clip, then once we've got him talking we'll drop Yuri into the conversation and say he told us to go there.'

She nodded, slipped her hand in her boot, unclipped the tie-clip from the side of her sock and walked inside. My phone rang. It was Bailey again. Jackson must really be piling on the pressure. I shoved it back in my jeans, put Oz on the lead and dragged him in after her. We had to weave our way through mountains of junk before we got to a man in a ratty armchair with a fag in one hand and the paper in the other. If this was Marty he was fat all right. His grubby brown shirt was the size of a tent and the buttons looked like they were about to burst. He glanced up.

'What do you want?'

'To sell something,' Nina said.

'Oh yeah?'

She held out the tie-clip. He looked from her to me, put down his fag and paper and, with a surprisingly delicate snap of his nicotine-stained fingers, took it from her. Then he screwed a little lens thing into his eye socket, adjusted the lamp beside him and started inspecting the tie-clip from every angle. After a second or two he craned forward, pursing his lips and breathing through his nose, the way people do when they're concentrating hard. He took out the lens, looked up at Nina and said, 'Where'd you get this?'

'That does not matter.'

His lip curled. 'I'll give you fifty quid.'

'No. That is very bad price. It is real gold and real diamond.'

'That's as maybe but there's not much call for this kind of thing, 'specially when the seller's being cagey about where they got it. But I'll do you a favour. I'll make it seventy-five.'

'It's worth loads more than that,' I said, 'and we've got a friend who said he sold some jewellery here and that you gave him a good price no questions asked.'

'Did he now?' His eyes narrowed so much they nearly disappeared into his flabby face.

'Yes and we kind of lost touch with him and we're trying to track him down. Maybe you remember him,' I held out Yuri's prison ID. 'He looks a bit older than this now.'

He glanced at the photo and grinned. 'Doing time can do that to you. 'Specially if you're banged up in one of them foreign jails.'

'So, you remember him coming in?' I said.

He picked up his fag and tapped a worm of ash on to the floor. 'I couldn't say. It's my brother Robbie you'd want to ask. He usually deals with the jewellery side of things. I tell you what, leave this tie-clip with me and as soon he gets back I'll get him to have a look at it and see what he can do price-wise.'

'No thanks,' I said quickly. 'We'll take it with us. How long will he be?'

''Bout an hour.'

'We'll come back.'

Nina tugged the tie-clip out of his hand and we made for the exit.

'Make sure you do,' Fat Marty called. 'You never know, if you make it worth his while, Robbie might even remember your mate.'

I shut the door behind us.

'I am sure he recognised Yuri's face,' Nina whispered, fixing the tie-clip back on her sock.

Half of me wanted to agree with her. The other half was scared of getting my hopes up. 'He was dead shifty, that's for sure. But I couldn't work out if he was just trying to rip us off or if there was something else going on. Let's get some food then we'll go back and see what his brother says.'

We cut through the back roads till we found a greasy spoon tucked down a little lane near the High Street. It wasn't just the spoons in that caff that were greasy. Everything, from the fogged-up windows and cracked formica tables to the red-faced woman behind the counter, was coated in a shiny layer of fat. Even the air felt sticky. But at least the management weren't fussed about customers bringing dogs in. It wasn't very busy, just a bloke in overalls getting a sausage roll and a takeaway tea, and an old couple sharing a round of toast. While I was at the counter ordering two all-day breakfasts my phone beeped again. My guts jumped. It was a text from Jackson. I felt sick. But it didn't last long.

Hey kid sorry I dissed u comin to catford to help where r u?

Jackson had to be feeling bad because he never apologised, never called anyone kid and, if he could help it, never set foot in South London.

Feeling like a twenty-ton weight had been lifted off my mind, I texted back.

julies caff swains lane off hi street.

Things were looking up. If Fat Marty and his brother did know anything about Yuri, Jackson would know exactly how to get it out of them. All I had to do now was convince Nina she could trust him.

Even the way Jackson drove I reckoned it would take him a while to get across London and I decided to let her chill for a bit before I broke the news. She'd picked the table furthest from the window and she was sitting with her head down and her back to the street. I brought over the teas and sat next to her. Once we'd gone over everything Fat Marty had said we took turns trying to guess how much the tie-pin was really worth.

The old couple toddled off just as our fry-ups arrived, and as Nina bent down to give Oz a bit of bacon I reached for the ketchup. It was in one of those plastic dispensers, the kind that looks like a fake tomato, and I'd got it upside down, squeezing it and thwacking it, trying to unblock the spout, when a blast of cold air hit my neck and some more customers strolled in. I caught a waft of sweat and cigarette smoke as a huge bloke in a leather jacket brushed past our table, on his way to the counter. He had this funny rolling walk and thick, muscly arms that were a bit too short for his barrel-shaped body. I whispered to Nina that from the back he reminded me of Shrek. He must have ordered something special because the red-faced woman looked a bit surprised, dropped the cup she was drying and disappeared out back.

As I gave the fake tomato another thump, a black-gloved hand shoved a ketchup bottle over my shoulder and a gruff voice said, 'Here, try this, Erroll. Or is it Joe?'

Next thing I know Viktor Kozek's got me by the hair and Shrek's lunging at Nina, shaking her like he's emptying a sack of potatoes and screaming at her in Russian.

'Leave her alone!' I yelled.

Kozek whacked me round the head, shooting fire through my brain. As they dragged us outside I reached wildly for Oz, but my world was exploding into splinters and he was just a blurry white streak and a jangle of echoey barks. Viktor clamped his arm around me, like I was sick and he was helping me to walk, and Shrek did the same with Nina, not that any of the passers-by seemed to notice or care. Two cars floated into focus, a black Lexus with Bogdan at the wheel and the flash Jeep I'd seen cruising down the High Street. I got a glimpse of Shrek's face and recognised the show-off who'd been driving it. He pushed Nina into the back of the Lexus, pounding her with his fists. She crumpled into the footwell, shaking, crying, pleading, bleeding.

'Stop it!' I screamed. 'She hasn't done anything. I just bumped into her in the caff.'

'Save your breath,' Viktor growled. 'He doesn't speak English.'

He shoved me in after her, landing his foot on my back, squishing my nose into the carpet and working grit into my mouth. I heard laughter. Coughing and spitting, I twisted round towards the window and caught Shrek heading for the Jeep. He was dangling Oz by his collar, grinning into his face and mimicking his frenzied yelps. Viktor was lounging back in his seat holding the photo of Yuri.

'You two think you're pretty smart, don't you? Only you're not smart enough. Yuri's nowhere near Catford. He's hiding out in East London. I've got people picking him up right now.'

'So let us go.'

'Why would I do that when I've got a very important client who's just dying to meet you?'

'Let Nina go. She didn't want to help me. I forced her.'

He laughed. Then his face turned stony. 'She knows the score. You cross Viktor Kozek, you pay the price.' His foot jabbed into her side. She was hunched so far down that I couldn't see her face but I heard her gasp. 'Anyway, I'm sure my client will want to know exactly who Nina has told about our friend Yuri.'

'Who . . . who is your client?'

'They call her the Vulture.' He grinned. 'They say she likes her victims dead before she picks them clean of everything they've got. And she knows plenty about you already. Real name – Joe Slattery. Mother killed in a car crash. Doesn't know when to mind his own business. That is you, isn't it?' He yanked my head back. 'Well?'

I wanted to shout at him and tell him he was slime, but I just whimpered a pathetic 'Yeah. That's me.'

He let go and smiled. 'I suppose I should be thanking

you for the tip-off about Yuri. It's not often a kid walks into my office and puts me on to a deal worth a million pounds.'

I sucked in a gulp of air and let it out as slow as I could, trying to control my voice. 'Why did she kill Sadie Slattery?'

He shrugged. 'I don't know and I don't want to know. Inquiring too closely into the Vulture's business isn't good for your health. But if you care that much you can ask her yourself. She's coming over to deal with you and Yuri in person.'

Excitement welled up through the pain and terror. If I didn't get out of this alive at least I'd get the chance to look Mum's killer in the eye before I died.

CHAPTER 18

Viktor had done talking. The next time I raised my head, one of his snakeskin boots squashed it into the carpet. OK, so I should have been counting every bump and turn, working out where we were headed. But you try driving anywhere scared witless, with your face rammed into the floor and every brake squeal triggering nightmare flashes of the car crash that killed your mum. Add in the sickening sway of the suspension and it was all I could do not to throw up and drown in my own puke. So it could have been one hour or five, ten miles or fifty by the time the car slowed, nosed sharply downhill and stopped. The clang of iron gates as the car edged forward notched up the fear to a whole new level.

They dragged us out into some kind of goods yard cluttered with rusty car carcasses, discarded machine parts and massive iron freight containers stacked up like giant Lego. The gates slammed behind us. I spun round and took in a fifteen-foot chain-link fence topped with razor wire, a grimy old caravan and a dented limo with shattered headlamps, up on blocks, before spotting Shrek hurling a whimpering Oz into a fenced-off area packed with gas canisters and old tyres.

Bogdan pushed me against the limo, emptied my pockets and tossed my phone to Viktor. Then he searched Nina, slapping her and yelling. She didn't seem to hear him, just stood there, head lolling on her chest, blood trickling from her lips. He wouldn't stop. A scary feeling blacker than anger took me over. The only Russian I knew was that *you filthy scum, I'll kill you* stuff that Yuri had been yelling in his sleep but right then it summed up exactly how I felt about Bogdan.

'*Ty gneeda paganaya* !' I shouted. '*Ya zamochoo tebya*.'

Bogdan swung round. His rubbery face contorted and he burst into heaving snorts of laughter like he'd heard the funniest joke in the world. Just as suddenly he whacked me so hard I thought he'd broken my jaw.

Through the blinding pain I heard Shrek and Viktor laughing, too, and saw Bogdan's fist clench to take another swing at me. Viktor snapped an order. Bogdan scowled and dropped his hand. Viktor obviously didn't want him spoiling the Vulture's fun by pulping me before she got there. My phone beeped in Viktor's hand. He checked the text and shoved the screen in my face. It was from Bailey. I blinked hard. The words wobbled into focus.

Where r u call me urgent.

I looked away. Viktor pinched my throbbing cheeks together with one hand and jerked my head round. 'Who's Bailey?'

The mist cleared a bit. If he didn't know who Bailey was, that was the way I was going to keep it. I groped for a lie.

'He's my . . . uncle . . .' Tiny scraps of a plan were floating round my head, coming together then falling apart when I tried to grab hold of them. 'He runs the off-licence next to the flats. He looks out for me.'

'What's he want you for?' Viktor demanded.

Don't lose it, Joe, keep going . . .

'I . . . stack crates for him. I was s'posed to do a shift this afternoon.'

My phone beeped again. His lip curled. 'Your uncle's getting anxious.'

Come on, Joe, this is your one chance to let Bailey know you're in trouble . . . don't blow it.

'He's . . . he's an ex-cop. I told him I was going to Catford . . . to help a mate track down some stolen gear. He warned me there might be trouble.'

Slow down. Don't overdo it.

'If I don't turn up he might . . . call his mates at the cop shop . . . so maybe I should . . . um . . . text him back.'

My acting was about as convincing as a picture of Elvis on a slice of burnt toast but I could see from his eyes that Viktor's nasty brain was weighing this up. I pushed it some more.

'If they check the CCTV and see you hustling us into your cars they might trace where you've taken us.'

I was guessing that Viktor had enough bent lawyers on his payroll not to worry about a couple of cops sniffing round but he definitely wouldn't want anything disturbing the Vulture's visit. He eyeballed me for a bit then he grunted and said, 'So we tell him you're OK.'

Yes! The first tiny bit of plan had worked but I couldn't see Viktor letting me follow it up by texting 'Help I've been kidnapped.' *Think of something that Bailey will get and Viktor won't. You can do this.* My skull ached with the effort of whizzing through lyrics, jokes, movies, catchphrases, books, characters – I spooled back, breathing fast. *Got it!*

I reached for the handset. Viktor jerked it away. 'I will write it. What shall I say?' One minute it was like he was asking me what to put on his nan's birthday card, the next he was slamming me in the stomach, screaming, 'I said, what shall I say?'

Stunned by the pain I could barely squeeze enough air out to speak. 'Put "Sorry Uncle Balfour, Can't come today . . . Ebenezer sick."'

'Balfour? Ebenezer?'

'Balfour Bailey – that's my uncle's name. And Ebenezer's my . . . dog . . .'

I watched him key in the words and press send, feeling a tiny twitch of triumph. I don't know why. Even if Bailey cracked my coded message what was he going to do about it, stuck on his couch without a clue where I was?

Viktor stumped off to the caravan leaving us in the loving care of Shrek and Bogdan who hauled us over to one of the containers. My heart emptied. Bogdan pushed up the horizontal locking bar, jerked open the doors and shoved us inside. I tripped and turned. A flash of the outside world cut the darkness before the door slammed, the locking bar clamped shut and we were swallowed up by blackness and the choking stench of vomit, pee, and rotting food.

I reached for Nina, struggling to prop her slumped body against the wall. Somewhere at the back of that stinking box I'd glimpsed dark shapes littering the floor. I stumbled towards them, waving my hands about till I touched the musty softness of a pile of cardboard packing cases, empty except for what felt like a couple of dresses still on their hangers. I stamped one of the biggest boxes flat to give her something to lie on and rolled the dresses into a damp, smelly pillow. She keeled over and lay there, not making a sound.

'You OK?' I whispered.

No answer. I shook her shoulder, desperate to hear another voice in that black, stinking silence.

'Come on, Nina. Speak to me.'

'This is . . . how they do it,' she breathed.

'Do what?'

'Smuggle people.'

'You can't carry *people* in one of these.'

'It is huge business for Viktor. Many people who want new life give him all their money. Then he packs them in box like this and puts it on ship or lorry. It is dark. They run out of food and water. They cannot breathe. But he does not care if they die.'

The darkness closed in. The air was getting heavier. I tried channel hopping in my head but the horrible scene

Nina had just described was jamming all networks. A scream crawled up the inside of my throat. I shut my eyes and clamped my jaws, pushing my fist against my mouth. The scream pushed back, fighting to get out. A sound like scuttling rats rustled the cardboard. I pulled in my legs, unable to bear it, unable to breathe. *If I'm going to die, please, please don't let it be like this.*

With a superhuman effort I bit on the scream and forced my eyes open. A milky glow was spotlighting Nina's thin bruised face, filtering up from the phone she'd got cupped in her hands. It was only a feeble gleam but it blew away the terror just like one of those night lights Mum used to get me as a kid.

'How d'you manage that?' I said.

'Hid it in my boot.'

I think she was trying to smile. The blood caked round her lips made it difficult to tell. Her eyes met mine, dazed and glassy.

'Who do we call, Joe? Not police, they will put my father in prison. What about . . . Jackson?'

His text flashed in my head.

Jackson: comin to catford to help where r u?

Reply: julies caff swains lane off hi street.

He'd set me up! Jackson Duval had set me up! What was left of my world was closing down. All along I'd been kidding myself that Jackson was like family, which just about summed up my pathetic excuse for a life. Joe Slattery, the waste of space whose so-called mate was ready to sell him out to evil trash like Viktor Kozek.

Footsteps sounded outside, the locking bar slid

upwards with a clunk, and Shrek, Viktor and Bogdan barged in. As I threw myself across Nina, Shrek caught me in a car-crusher grip and hurled me across the container. Spitting a mouthful of ugly sounds in Nina's face Viktor threw her phone on the floor, smashed it under his heel and raised his hand to strike her. I lunged for his arm and got a back-handed slap across the mouth from Bogdan. It was only a flick, like swatting a fly, but it banged me back against the wall with the force of a wrecking ball.

Viktor was pulling up Nina's crumpled body, ready to lay into her, when his own phone went off, filling the container with the screechy wail of a girl band, which would have been funny if I hadn't been terrified and coughing blood.

He answered it with a grunt, listened for barely a moment then spewed out a stream of furious Russian, firing half of it down the handset and the rest at Shrek and Bogdan. Within seconds all three of them were out of there. The doors slammed and the locking bar clamped down, sealing us in. Outside, engines revved, gravel crunched and the iron gates clanged shut. Inside, Nina started making this weird bleating noise.

'What was that about?' I gasped.

'Yuri. They found him in East London, down near Olympic Park. But he got away.'

'Is that where they've gone?'

'Yes. To help find him. Viktor wants his million pounds.'

I shut my eyes, willing Yuri to get away.

'What if something happens and they don't come back?'

'Then we will suffocate or die of thirst.'

Her words dried all the spit in my mouth and brought back the panic.

Keep it together, Joe. Give up now and you're dead.

CHAPTER 19

Nina had gone quiet and when I touched her she was curled up stiff like a dead thing.

'I do not feel good, Joe,' she whispered.

'What hurts?'

'Everything. I think Bogdan broke my rib.'

I had to get us out of there. I did a fingertip search of the walls, hoping for a loose panel or a hidden hatch, and ended up punching the cold, sealed panels till they rang. Hating the thick dirty darkness, I threw my weight against the doors, detonating fresh explosions of pain down my side. I moved on, kicking cardboard, sending a coat hanger twanging across the floor and stretching up to test every inch of reachable space. After a complete circuit I sank down next to Nina.

'Anything?' she said.

'Nope.'

I took stock. It wasn't looking good. But when you're banged up in a tin coffin, hurting all over and waiting your turn to get worked over by a psycho crime boss, it's funny how it's the little things that get to you. Like, and this is just 'for instance', how come Viktor walked in the minute Nina got her phone out? I ran that by her. She didn't speak.

'Nina?'

'I heard you. I am thinking.'

'And?'

Groaning, she pulled herself upright. 'They are filming us.'

'How?'

'There must be night-vision camera in here.'

I had the feeling Viktor got regular use out of this little holding cell so a camera made sense. In fact, I could just see him lolling back on one of his velvet chairs, downing beers and watching re-runs of his favourite interrogations on that giant screen in his office.

I flicked to a re-run of my own – the view I'd got of the container just before they shoved us inside. It's amazing how desperation sharpens your mind. By stopping breathing and blanking everything else I got it into focus. Nine or ten feet high, eight or so feet wide, peeling brown paintwork rusted round the base, a silver locking bar running horizontally across the double doors. And . . . tucked under the roof, a little black box with a grey, plastic-coated wire poking out the back and trailing down the side.

'It's above the doors, slightly to the right,' I said.

'How do you know this?'

'I saw the wiring outside. Check if you want. Stand on my back.'

I got on all fours. Breathing in short, painful gasps, she climbed up, light as a bag of rags, and all I could think of was Bogdan's huge fist smashing into her skinny frame.

'I have got it,' she said from the darkness above me. 'Stay still . . . Yes. It is thermal for seeing in dark – no lens, just heat sensitive plate. My father, he installs these sometimes.' She made a funny little sound. 'Maybe he installed this one.'

We braced ourselves for one of Viktor's thugs to come running in to stop us messing with it. Nothing. They'd all gone to find Yuri. But if they found him how long would we have before the Vulture turned up and started her interrogation?

We huddled in the blackness thinking about that camera capturing thermal images of our long slow deaths if no one came back for us, or our quicker, more agonising ones if they did. Telly programmes about hostage situations always go on about keeping your spirits up, which is fine if you're in a TV studio. Not so easy if you're sitting in the pitch black and it's your spirits that are spiralling into freefall. They got one thing right though, silence is a killer. Nina was all out of small talk and the only thing I could think of to say was, 'You seem pretty clued up about your dad's work.'

She took a while to answer. 'I had reasons for learning.' For all she was so shaky there was a definite hint of pride in her voice.

'Am I missing something here?' I said.

'How do you think I know so much about Viktor's business?'

'I had wondered.'

'I used my father's equipment to bug his office. I hoped that if I got enough – what is word – dirt on him, one day I would find way to use it.'

She wasn't bragging, just telling it like it was. No wonder she'd scoffed at my pathetic attempt to bug her with my phone.

'You won't get the chance if we die in here,' I said, searching my pockets. 'Maybe we can unscrew the camera and let in some air. You got a coin?'

I felt her lean forward and fiddle with her boot. 'No, but I have still got tie-clip.'

Right then I'd have swapped all the diamond tie-clips in the world for a screwdriver. But it was better than nothing.

I dropped back on all fours. Unsteadily, Nina heaved herself up and poked around in the dark, her breathing getting scratchier by the minute.

'The camera is on bracket but I can only reach one screw and I cannot make it turn.' She toppled off. 'You must do it.'

She handed me the tie-clip and I felt her curling into a crouch. Kicking off my trainers I prodded her back with my toe, gentle as I could. Her spine felt bony and brittle, like it was about to snap. She let out a hiss of pain.

I jerked my foot away. 'I can't. I'll break you in two.'

'Do it, Joe.'

So I stood on her back and fumbled in the dark, working my stiff cold fingers in quick bursts and stepping down every few minutes to give her a break. The end of the tie-clip was too thin to be any use but wedging the longer side in the screw slots and jerking it round bit by bit for what seemed like hours got three of the screws undone. A hard twist loosened the fourth. I gave the bracket a tug, and a shaft of light punctured the darkness as it fell forward with the camera, still attached, dangling from its cable. With a whoop I leapt off Nina's back. She rolled over, gasping for breath. For all the blood round her mouth she was definitely smiling this time.

If you've never been locked up in a dark, airless box you'll never understand how beautiful that little round hole looked to us, or how good it felt to cross suffocation off the list of ways we were going to die. OK, so it still left plenty of alternatives but that wasn't the point.

My brain hit rewind again, playing back the sight and sound of Shrek's fat fingers slamming down the locking bar and the grating thud of clamping metal. *Slam clunk, slam clunk.* I played it over and over, trying to take in the details. The locking bar was roughly the height of his chest and the pressure he'd used had barely rippled the muscles of his thick neck. *Slam clunk. Slam clunk.*

A crazy idea crept into my mind. I lurched round in the gloom, seized on the coat hanger and started unbending the stiff metal till I had a long straight-ish piece of wire with a hook at one end.

Nina watched me, puzzled. 'What are you doing?'

'You're going to use this to pull up the locking bar.'

'Me?' She shook her head. 'You are taller *and* stronger.'

Holding her breath, she let me clamber on her back again, barely buckling when I got her to raise herself higher so I could double check there was no one patrolling the yard. It was deserted. Beyond the wire fence a steep ridge sloped up to a line of tall, skinny trees that flickered as a lone car sped along the road behind. The only sound was Oz's furious yapping from the tyre store.

Slowly, I fed the wire through the hole. Trouble was, this job called for precision and I was working blind, with three fingers squeezed into a space the size of a tea cup, with nothing to guide me but the clink of the hanger bouncing off the bar. The wire kept slipping, my fingers were going numb and Nina was gasping that she couldn't take it much longer. Then the hook bit. For a second I understood the obsession people get with fishing. I jerked hard and felt the bar give, just a little. Gripping the taut wire I tugged again. Something slackened. The hook was uncurling. Swearing loudly I shifted my fingers to yank the wire back inside, lost hold and heard it clatter on to the yard.

Game over.

I jumped off Nina's back and slithered into a heap beside her. If there'd been any one out there who cared if I lived or died I'd have scratched a goodbye message on the wall. Instead, I handed Nina the tie-clip and told her to write something to her mum and dad.

She threw me this annoyed frown, grabbed the dangling bracket and started unscrewing the little nuts and bolts that fixed it to the camera. Once the bracket was free she held it up. It was a heavy strip of metal, about an inch wide and L-shaped. 'If we make smaller we can use this as hook,' she said.

Game on again.

I took the bracket and stamped it into more of a V-shape. 'We can use our belts to lower it down,' I said, trying to sound like I'd never lost the will to live.

Her belt was thin white plastic; mine was leather but badly worn. I buckled them together, worried how much strain they could take and began to wonder the same about me and Nina. We used a screw and nut to fix the belts to the bracket and stood back to admire our handiwork. It didn't look like much but it was all that stood between us and death. Nina was pale and trembly, too weak to stand up straight, let alone take my weight again.

'You do it,' I said.

She shook her head and got down in a crouch. If willpower was all it took to survive, Nina was in there with a chance. I wound the end of her belt tight round my hand, stepped on her back and passed the bracket out through the hole, with the angle facing away from the container. Carefully, I fed the belts out after it, inch by inch until our DIY grappling hook just *had* to be hanging lower than the bar.

'OK. Here goes.' I closed my fingers tight round the belts and wrenched with both hands. The bracket caught. I heard it. My heart leapt. The locking bar didn't move. I pulled again straining every muscle. Nothing.

'I cannot . . .' Nina groaned. Her body shuddered. She swayed for a moment and collapsed, leaving me strung up like a pig on a butcher's hook, my weight pulling the tightly wound belt so hard it stopped the blood in my hand and nearly wrenched my shoulder out of its socket. I yelled in agony, trying to jerk my fingers free. Suddenly the excruciating pressure released. A length of belt slithered through the hole, my feet hit the floor and with a beautiful clunk, the locking bar lifted. For one long, gobsmacked moment we stared at the strip of silver between the door panels before I kicked them open, letting in a flood of dirty grey light. I tore off the belt, and, flexing my throbbing palm, I burst across the yard to free Oz, who stalked past me in a strop when he saw I hadn't brought him any food.

Nina made straight for the caravan, panting with pain as she ran. She peered through the window and tried the door. It was locked, so get this, she picked up a brick and chucked it through the window. She blushed when she saw me staring.

'Don't mind me,' I said. Reaching for another brick, I knocked away the splinters of glass round the edge. She folded her hoodie, wedging it across the frame and made me give her a leg-up so she could scramble inside. Two seconds later she was opening the door and letting me and Oz into a poky little space that stank of alcohol, chips and sweat. The telly on the table was tuned to a gripping shot of the floor of the shipping container, glowing flickery and green like a cheap horror movie on account of the thermal imaging. I turned on the tap and sucked at the trickle of tepid water while Nina rummaged through the fridge and cupboards. Except for a couple of squares of chocolate, a mildewed loaf and a squidgy black banana it was just beer, vodka and a mountain of empty take-out boxes. She handed me half the chocolate and poured some water into a foil container for Oz.

'What do we do now?' she said, wetting her hand and wiping the worst of the blood off her face.

'Stay here.' I left her trying to tempt Oz with the banana and did a quick recce of the yard. The gate was the only way out and that was fifteen feet high and locked. I ran back to the caravan.

'Tools,' I said. 'Look for anything we can use to cut the fence.'

We hunted through the garbage, pulling open every drawer and cupboard. I heard her gasp. She reached between the beer bottles and fished something out. With a tiny crooked smile she held it out to me. It was a bottle opener attached to a Swiss army knife. I ripped my nail digging out the folding pliers attachment and told her to keep searching while I checked the fence for weak points.

The mesh was thick and heavy, stretched tightly between sturdy metal posts cemented into the ground, except for one place at the far end where it looked like a car had backed up, busted a couple of links and bent one of the posts. Trying not to worry about the fading light, I knelt down and got on with it, using the tiny pliers to gnaw at the damaged wires. From across the yard a car boot slammed.

'Any luck?' I shouted.

'Maybe. I find tool box. No cutters for wire though.'

Physically, Nina was built like a dragonfly, mentally she

was pure steel. It was amazing the way she ignored the pain in her ribs and set to with a hacksaw blade. We got into a bit of a rhythm, snipping and sawing. Even so, it took us ages to cut a flap the size of a cereal box. Oz squeezed through it a couple of times and I had to shout to get him to come back.

After we'd cut six more links in each direction the gap was looking more promising. Spurred on, we were working like crazy when Nina let out a shriek and yanked her hand back. I spun round, shocked by the panic in her voice. Blood was gushing out of the deep cut she'd sliced through the curve of skin between her thumb and forefinger.

I ripped a strip off the bottom of my grubby T-shirt, trying not to think about tetanus, lockjaw and blood poisoning. She must have cut through a vein or an artery or something because the blood kept coming thick and red even though I was winding the bandage as tight as I could. Reaching out to steady herself she glanced over my shoulder.

'Joe. They are back!'

I looked round. Up on the ridge two sets of headlights were swinging off the road and bouncing down the track to the gate. We had to hide. Fast. I hauled Nina across the yard, tugged open the door of the broken-down limo, pushed her on to the back seat and scrambled after her, reaching up a finger to ease the locks shut. I strained my ears for Yuri's voice, wondering if they'd caught him, praying that they hadn't. Nina raised herself up to look through the window.

'Get down!' I hissed.

'It is OK. It is tinted glass.'

Feeling stupid I got up beside her. They'd seen the gaping door of the container and screeched the Jeep and the Lexus to a halt in the open gateway, engines running, doors flung wide. Viktor, Shrek and Bogdan piled out and tore off in different directions, kicking doors, racing round the caravan and smashing packing cases with Oz barking at their heels like it was some kind of game.

I was tempted to laugh till Shrek got out a gun.

Bogdan ran past the limo, looming close enough to see the acne on his cheeks. Suddenly the white glare of floodlights lit up the yard and the whole surrounding slope, like an alien space ship was landing. If we'd made a run for it through the gate they'd have picked us off like ants.

In the glow filtering through the tinted windows Nina looked like a ghost, her face drained grey by the blood spreading across her jeans. I squeezed her wrist, trying to stop the flow. *Make a plan, Joe. Make a plan.* Why hadn't I listened to Mum when she wanted me to join the boy scouts?

The good news was that I couldn't see Yuri. The bad news was that Nina was bleeding to death.

CHAPTER 20

Viktor, Bogdan and Shrek were tearing through the yard like a pack of starving sharks. Any minute now they'd get to the limo. *Come on, Joe. Think. Think.*

I'd been petrified Oz was going to give us away but a couple of sharp kicks from Bogdan had sent him flying towards the gate. I could see he was hurt and I felt bad I couldn't help him but he suddenly seemed to perk up and started snuffling round the Lexus, getting more and more excited till he finally jumped inside. If they'd got another takeaway in there I didn't fancy their chances of finding much of it left.

I stared at the cars parked there in the open gateway – lights on, engines running, doors open – and froze, torn between the crazy escape plan storming my brain and the picture of Mum getting smashed up in Lincoln's Renault.

One glance at the blood pumping out of Nina's hand made up my mind.

'I'm going to steal the Lexus,' I said.

Considering how little we had going for us I thought the plan was pretty inspired. All Nina said was, 'You can drive?'

'Yeah . . . kind of.' It wasn't a lie, not really.

She blinked a bit but didn't come up with a better idea. I flicked up the blade of the Swiss army knife.

'Keep your head down and stay low. Ready?'

Nina nodded. I unlocked the door, dropped to the ground and lifted her down. Pulling her by her good hand, I crept along the side of the limo, peeked round the battered bonnet and saw them circling the far end of the yard.

'Now,' I hissed. We ran for the Lexus. Shoving her in the passenger seat I sneaked towards the Jeep and managed to plunge the blade into both of its nearside tyres before Viktor found the hole in the wire mesh, let out a bellow like a wounded moose and led a dash for the cars. I dived for the Lexus. It was an automatic. D for Drive, R for reverse – right? I bloody hoped so.

I dropped the hand brake, rammed the selector to R and floored the accelerator. We shot backwards through the gateway. Shrek lumbered into the light and fired off a round in our direction. I swung the car in a circle. It was like riding the sickest roller coaster ever. The ground veered up and the door clipped a tree before I managed to pull it shut. I hit D, revved the engine and made for the top of the slope. Shrek fired again, hitting the bumper. I peeled off the track on to tarmac, hurtling down the wrong side of the road. A lorry roared towards us blaring its horn ... *Je-sus*! I swerved into the other lane struggling to steady the car as the world whizzed past. Locking my eyes on the road, I gripped the wheel as if my fingers were welded to the plastic but a few spins round the estate with the Farm Street joyriders and a life-long addiction to video games were no preparation for hitting the road in a tank-sized Lexus. I yelled at Nina to get the sat nav working. She reached a shaky hand towards the screen.

'Find where we are. Check the nearest hospital,' I said.

After a bit she said, 'Essex,' in a weird spacey voice. 'Nearest hospital . . . five miles. But we cannot stop.'

She had a point. Who knew how quickly Viktor could call up more cars and come looking for us? But if she was going to make it we'd have to risk it. I reached over, hit 'confirm' on the sat nav and floored the accelerator.

'Tighten the bandage. Hold your arm up.' I ordered, though I wasn't sure if gravity worked on blood.

Trying to hold the Lexus steady and keep a look-out for Viktor was a nightmare. Every time I checked the mirrors the car swerved, or some random truck roared out of nowhere nearly blinding me. The sat nav sent us left. I pulled hard on the wheel. The car veered violently, bumping and scraping the kerb as we screeched on to a dual carriageway. Nina crumpled down in her seat, her eyes fluttering like she was slipping out of consciousness. I kept yelling at her, clutching her wrist, squeezing it hard, then dropping it to grab the wheel again, panicking every time I caught headlights in the mirror. The bossy voice of the sat nav was the only thing keeping me going till a sign saying 'Hospital' loomed out of the night. I skidded into the car park and pulled Nina out. Oz tried to come too but I pushed him back and told him to lie down and keep quiet.

Somehow I managed to half-drag, half-carry Nina into Accident and Emergency. Considering how much I hated hospitals, it was pretty ironic how much time I was spending in them. I pulled her through the doors, steeling myself for the sounds and smells that I knew were going to trigger the dark memories of the night Mum died. But now they were mixed up with pictures of Prof Lincoln hanging between life and death in intensive care and visions of what was going to happen to Nina if she lost any more blood. And it was all because of that evil psycho witch who called herself the Vulture.

I pushed through the crush of people and laid Nina across a row of chairs. She'd gone totally limp and just lay there eyes half closed, covered in blood. I looked round wildly. A couple of nurses came towards us, not running but moving fast.

'It's her hand,' I gasped. 'It won't stop bleeding. She sliced it with a saw and she keeps passing out.'

The nurse grimaced as she untied the grimy blood-soaked strip of T-shirt. 'All right. We'll make her a priority. What's her name?'

Nina groaned and her eyes half-opened, darting me a

warning. I'd forgotten. She was illegal, no right to be here, maybe no right to treatment either.

'Sadie,' I said quickly. 'Her name's Sadie Slattery.'

'Give reception the rest of her details.'

I lied some more to the receptionist, giving her Doreen's address, my date of birth and pretending that Nina's aunty was parking the car and would be along any minute to sign the forms.

I sat down, dizzy with relief that Nina was being taken care of, petrified that Viktor's thugs were going to storm in any minute and woozy with hunger. All I'd had in the last eight hours was a bite of chocolate, a slurp of tap water and an overdose of adrenalin. I headed for the vending machines and started stabbing the coin return buttons in the hope of scraping up enough money to buy a packet of crisps. No luck. I lurched back to my seat and as I dropped my head in my hands almost ready to cry, I got that tight itchy feeling in my scalp. Someone was watching me. I looked up warily and caught the probing stare of a burly black guy sitting across the aisle. He had a slash on his cheek and looked like he'd just finished one argument and was up for another. He wasn't Ukrainian, that was for sure, but he was striding towards me, one hand stuffed in his pocket like he'd got a gun or a knife in there. I shrank back. He whipped out his fist. My heart jack-knifed. His fingers opened and a handful of coins bounced into my lap. Mainly coppers but one or two pound coins and a few fifty, ten, and twenty-pence pieces.

'Looks like you could do with a snack,' he growled.

I stared up at him, shocked and grateful.

'You'll never know,' I croaked.

'Been there a few times myself.'

The big guy clenched his fist again and touched mine. As he went back to his seat a nurse called out 'Ronan Bellfield' and he picked up a battered guitar and disappeared through the swing doors.

I fed the money into the vending machines, wondering how many songs he'd had to sing to buy me that cheese sandwich and that bottle of Coke. I divided the sandwich into three pieces and ate mine hunched in a corner with one eye on the swing doors watching for Nina, and the other on the entrance in case Viktor, Bogdan or Shrek turned up. My nerves were in shreds. What was taking so long?

Finally she came out. She'd got her hand in a sling and she was walking without help but her clothes were still covered in blood and there were deep purple smudges under her eyes that stood out against the pasty white of her face.

I handed her a chunk of sandwich and the rest of the Coke. 'C'mon. Let's get out of here.'

'Sadie Slattery!'

Like an idiot I swung round, looking for Mum. A nurse was walking towards us holding up a little white packet. 'You forgot your pills, Sadie.'

I tried to ward off the pain by telling myself Mum would have been pleased that her name had come in handy.

'Take two every four hours,' the nurse said. 'And make

sure you rest that hand and take things easy.'

Take things easy. Yeah, right.

Sneaking into the half-empty car park we made a dive for the shadows and crouched by the wall, watching headlights criss-cross the tarmac as a straggle of nightshift workers came and went. I pressed the key remote. The Lexus squawked, flashing a response. We counted the seconds, waiting for Bogdan or Shrek to come running. Nothing. I made a move towards the Lexus. Nina grabbed my arm and went rigid.

'What's up?' I said.

'It was shock of cutting my hand. I was not thinking.'

'What d'you mean?'

'Viktor. He has tracking devices in all his cars. If he gets to computer he can follow us wherever we go.'

I scanned the parked cars, searching for one that would be old enough to hot wire. It was a toss-up between a beaten-up, soft-top Mini and a rusty white van. I picked the Mini. But when it came to the actual hot wiring I'd have to rely on my recall of the it's-so-easy-I-can-do-it-one-handed auto theft scenes I'd watched in a million movies and the time the Farm Street joyriders dared me to have a go at Eddy's Fiesta and I nearly got fried.

'Get Oz and keep a look out,' I said.

Nina scurried over to the Lexus, pulled Oz off the back seat and tried to drag him over to the Mini. He dug in, refusing to budge, and when she tried to pick him up he wriggled free and jumped up at the boot whining and clawing the paintwork.

'Oz, for God's sake, we haven't got time for this,' I hissed, running back and grabbing his collar.

Nina waved me quiet. 'Listen, Joe. There is something in there.'

Even with all the noise Oz was making I could hear a muffled thumping coming from the boot.

'Stand back.' I pressed the key fob. Slowly, the cover rose up like the lid of Dracula's coffin and the interior light clicked on. There was a huge bloke curled up inside, all wrapped in duct tape like a half-finished mummy with a black hood over his head.

'Je-sus!' I said.

Oz was going crazy so I threw his bit of sandwich on to the back seat, chucked him in after it and shut the door. Then I tugged the hood off the man's head. The first thing I saw was a bloody gash across his forehead. The second was a pair of black bloodshot eyes blinking up at me like I was some kind of angel in a vision.

It was Yuri.

Wrong time, wrong place to start asking all the questions I'd got backing up in my brain. But still . . .

Viktor's boys had done a thorough job of tying him up and without the Swiss army knife I'd never have got the tape off his arms and legs. He was totally out of it and it took me, Nina and a lot of heaving and pushing to get him out of the boot and lean him against the side of the Lexus.

I ran to the Mini, slit the soft top and reached inside for the handle. Groping under the dash I pulled out the tangle of cables, trying to work out which ones were the ignition and starter wires. It wasn't like this in the movies. I took a risk and flipped on the interior light, just for a second. *Keep calm, Joe, you can do this.* I picked out one red and one black wire, and used the pliers attachment to clip them and strip back the insulation. Bracing myself against the fifty-fifty chance of getting frazzled I twisted them together and gave a *yes* of triumph when the dashboard warning lights flickered on. As I fiddled around, the starter wire made contact and gave off a grudging spark. The ancient engine grunted and turned over. I fumbled with the clutch and crashed the gears. The car hiccoughed, lurched about two yards and stalled.

Hurrying to restart it, I saw Nina, lard white and scarecrow-haired, her clothes still covered in blood, trying to help Yuri towards the Mini. Bits of duct tape flapped from his clothes and he was swaying around, opening and closing his mouth like a landed trout. In the sickly yellow car park lights they looked like a couple of extras from *Night of the Living Dead*.

I pulled up beside them. Yuri was in a bad way and I only just managed to manoeuvre him on to the tiny back seat before he passed out. I ran to fetch Oz. By the time I got back Nina had taken off her sling and was sitting in the driver's seat wrapping the filthy hood we'd taken off Yuri round her own head in a kind of turban. Rather her than me, but it did the job of hiding her silvery hair.

'Put your sling back on and move over,' I said.

'I am driving,' she said. 'I have driven tractors, remember?'

'What about your stitches?'

She pulled a face. 'This car has gears. Even with one hand I will drive it better than you.'

'Thanks.'

But she was right and there was no point beating myself up about it. I got in the passenger seat, pulled Oz in after me and tossed her a pair of thick black-framed glasses I'd spotted on the dashboard.

Headlights swept the tarmac and a silver Volvo screeched to a stop in front of the Lexus. Viktor's tracking system had worked. Two big guys in leather jackets got out and opened the boot. As soon as they saw it was empty one of them got on his phone and started walking up and down, peering between the parked cars, while the other one struck off towards the entrance to A and E. A couple of nurses hurried past and a little Fiat pulled out of a space opposite.

'Go! Go now!' I hissed. 'He'll think you're one of the night staff going home.'

I rammed Oz into the footwell. He didn't like it but I crouched over, holding him down. Nina eased the car into first and puttered past the Lexus. I watched in the wing mirror as the bloke with the phone glanced round, looking for three people – an ash-blonde girl, a mixed-race boy and an old man trussed up like a chicken. What he saw was a woman in a dark hat and glasses, driving sedately towards the exit in a beaten-up Mini. What I saw was the stubbly face of the man who'd watched me smash up that over-the-top wreath on Mum's grave.

As soon as we hit the road Oz made an excited scramble into the back and hurled himself at Yuri, licking his face and prodding him with his paw. Nina pulled off the glasses and pumped the accelerator till she'd put at least a mile between us and the car park. Even though she was only using her left hand to change gear, the new bandage was already soggy with blood and her lips puckered in pain when she asked the question I'd been dreading.

'Where to?'

Good question, Nina. Farm Street was a total no-go and I couldn't see Doreen wheeling out the welcome wagon for a couple of blood-stained illegals on the run from the Ukrainian Mafia. As for the Besedka . . . . yeah well, let's just say that when it came to safe hiding places we weren't exactly spoilt for options.

'Find some woods. You can rest for a bit and I'll try to get some sense out of Yuri.'

I leant over the seat and tried to bring him round, slapping his face and dribbling Coke into his mouth. All he did was spit it out, thrash his legs and groan.

'Yuri. Wake up. Why's the Vulture after you? Why did she kill Ivo Lincoln and Sadie Slattery?' I slapped him harder. 'She was my mother, come on, tell me!'

Barely conscious, he just stared through me, mumbling in Russian.

'Nina! What's he saying?'

'That he would rather die than go on running.'

I was with him there. Suddenly Yuri lunged forward, gripped Nina 's shoulders and started shouting in her ear. The Mini swerved. Wincing with agony she slammed her bandaged hand on the wheel, struggling to regain control. I shoved Yuri back. 'Stop it! You'll get us all killed.'

Somewhere in his angry rant I picked out two words I recognised: *Elysium* and *Korshun*.

'What is it, Nina? What's he saying?'

'He is confused. Words are not clear but he says bad thing happened at Elysium and now he must make Vulture pay for what she did.'

It was like she'd punched a hole in the darkness. In the trickle of light I could see all the random bits of data I'd picked up about the Vulture flying together, building up a picture of real person. She was a powerful woman, obsessed with secrecy, rich enough to put a million quid on Yuri's head, ready to kill anyone who got in her way, and now he was saying she'd been involved in something bad at Elysium. Snatches of Norma Craig's voice kept breaking through, like interference on Mum's old radio, getting louder and clearer till they were all I could hear . . . *there are far more inhuman crimes than murder . . . when you do something truly terrible . . . The lies, the pretence, the guilt* . . . It was her! Norma Craig was the Vulture! Not Clairmont! This time it all fitted. Think about it. Norma, the daughter of a sixties gangster, Norma weighed down by guilt, Norma with her endless millions, flashy office and thirty-year blank on her CV. Sickest of all, Norma fixing it so she could meet me face to face and harp on about forgiveness. I'd thought she was crazy. But she was more than that. It was like she'd got a split personality, murdering Mum and Lincoln one minute, spilling her guts to me the next. Struggling to breathe, I seized Yuri's arms, trying to shake him awake. 'It's Norma, isn't it? Norma Craig is the Vulture!

His head jerked up and his eyes flickered open and shut as if they were wired to a faulty circuit. 'Miss Norma. Where is she? Where is Miss Norma?'

'At Elysium.'

'No. No. No.' He was slurring his words. 'House empty. She not there.'

'She came back. That's why the builders turned up. Remember? You had to get away. I've been looking for you ever since. Yuri, listen to me, the Vulture had Ivo Lincoln killed.'

He smiled a crazy smile. 'No. He help me. He write my story in newspaper. He tell everyone who Vulture really is.'

'No. He can't. He's dead!' I was talking loud and slow but it wasn't going in. 'She had him and my mother killed. In a car crash. Why did he go to see Sadie Slattery that night? What did she have to do with the Vulture?'

His peered at me as if I was the one talking gibberish. 'Sadie? Who is Sadie? I do not know Sadie.'

'She was my mother. She lived in Saxted as a kid. Is it something to do with her mother working for Norma Craig?'

'Miss Norma.' He punched his chest and gazed into the distance, as if he could see her coming. 'Take me to Miss Norma. If I can look in her eyes and tell her what is in my heart I do not care if they kill me.'

'Tell her what, Yuri?' I shook him hard.

His eyes rolled back and he drifted into unconsciousness. I let him go, feeling like I was going to burst. Every time I thought I'd found a way out of this weird maze of mirrors, I'd turn a corner and smash into my own reflection. I couldn't take it. I was sick of mysteries and even sicker of running.

'Stop the car!'

'What?' Nina pushed my hand off the wheel and screeched to a stop.

I fumbled for the last few coins I'd got left from the hospital. 'Take it. Go and wait in that bus shelter. If I can, I'll come back for you. If not, you'll still be better off than coming with us.'

'Coming where?'

'Elysium. Yuri wants to have it out with Norma Craig and so do I.'

'You are mad. If she is Vulture she will kill you.'

'Maybe. But first I'm going to make her tell me why she killed Mum.'

'Why would she tell you this?'

'She's a psycho but she's screwed up with guilt. If I can get her on her own, just her and me, like last time, I think I can get her to talk.'

'Then what will you do?'

'I don't know. I don't care.'

'She will have bodyguards everywhere.'

'No, at Elysium she's just got the one. Probably so no one susses she's leading a double life.'

'I come with you.'

'No.'

'You cannot even drive properly.' Nina revved the engine and swung back into the road. 'Besides, I have nowhere else to go.'

I glanced at her and saw her mouth set hard.

'OK. But you're going to wait in the woods.'

She drew up by a signpost that meant nothing to either of us.

'See if there is map,' she said.

There wasn't but I kind of knew that Essex was north of Kent so we should head south till we hit signs I recognised. The only problem was, which way was south?

I gazed into the night trying to remember this documentary that me and Mum had watched about an escaped POW who made his way across Europe navigating by the stars. That kind of stuff doesn't usually stick in my mind, but Mum had been writing a song about finding your way when things get tough, and having a bit of trouble with the lyrics. So we'd stood on our balcony and had a go at picking out the stars he'd used to guide him. But she still couldn't make the lyrics work. And she never did finish that song.

I poked my head out the window, stared up at the sky and told Nina to take a left as soon as she could. She thought I'd flipped till I told her about the documentary. She made a snorting noise and swung a left. I don't know which of us was more surprised when my plan finally started to work.

Between checking signposts and giving Nina directions I replayed my last meeting with Norma Craig. A dark, sticky anger bubbled up inside me, erupting in bursts of fury whenever I got to the bits where she'd looked me in the eye and talked about guilt and regret. But I knew I'd have to keep a lid on it when I got to

Elysium, at least for long enough to make her tell me why she ordered Mum's death. First I'd drop Mum into the conversation really casually then I'd draw the truth out of Norma bit by bit, like one of those cop-show psychologists. Once she'd confessed, somehow I'd find a way to make her pay for what she'd done. The struggle to hold back the hatred was waking me up, sharpening my brain, blocking out the hunger, pain and thirst. Which was good because Nina had started nodding off and if I hadn't kept prodding her, turning up the radio and opening the windows, we'd never have made it. As the Mini rumbled into Saxted woods and the floodlit outline of Elysium loomed through the gates she stiffened and stared up at the house, suddenly wide awake.

'What's wrong?' I said.

'That is Elysium?'

'Yeah, why?'

'Viktor has been watching CCTV of this house.'

'What? How?'

She frowned down at her hands. 'It has security cameras. My father cloned feeds. It is not difficult, Viktor makes him do it a lot.'

'I don't get it. Why's Viktor spying on the Vulture?'

'Probably to steal from her. He got my father to disconnect alarms in house as well.'

'Well, at least that's one less thing to worry about. The CCTV's going to be a problem though.'

'None of Viktor's people will be checking it tonight – they are all out looking for us.'

'Thanks for the reminder.'

I stumbled to the oak tree and felt around for the keys I'd hidden in the tangle of roots, freaking out till I found they'd slipped deeper than I'd thought. I ran back to the Mini and got Nina to follow the track around, pull up by the little door in the wall and turn off the headlights. I turned to check on Yuri, He was slumped in a twitching, groaning sleep. Oz jumped off his chest and scrambled for the door, tail thumping.

'Sorry, Oz. You've got to stay here with Yuri.'

He whimpered a bit but backed off when he sensed I was serious. I hunted around for the Swiss army knife, swearing loudly when I realised I must have dropped it in the hospital.

'What is plan?' Nina hissed.

'I'll go through that door, let myself into the house and surprise her. You wait here.'

'That is not plan.'

Said out loud it did seem a bit short on detail and I didn't put up much of a fight when she pitched out of the car, pulled off her turban and followed me through the back gate. Most of the lawns had been cleared but the garden was still edged by a shadowy border of chest-high shrubs and bushes that creaked and rustled in the wind. A light glimmered in the house, probably Norma Craig waiting up for news from Viktor.

'Joe, stay low, there are . . . '

I froze, blinded by a dazzling burst of light. Blinking with terror, I made a dash for the darkness, cringing behind the statue of a one-armed woman and watching a whole ring of security lights come on round the garden.

'I told you to stay low.' Nina was crouching under a bush, pointing up at a winking pinprick of red above the door.

'How long before they switch themselves off?' I hissed.

'A while. Do not move. If anyone looks out maybe they think it was foxes.'

I pressed my back against the ivy-covered stone, trying to stop my heart bursting through my chest, and shifting my eyes nervously from side to side. In the bright light I could see that someone had cleared all the brambles out of the greenhouse, replaced the glass and filled the shelves with tall spindly flowers in pots. To one side of the door was a new water butt with some garden tools propped against it.

A stick gave a warning crack. I spun round.

'Joe Slattery! I might have known bad blood would out. What were you going to do? Creep into the house and attack me in my bed?'

The sight of Norma Craig stepping from the trees, her silvery hair glittering and the red dragons on her silky black kimono fluttering, blitzed the careful speeches I'd planned. All I could hear was my heart pounding and my voice hissing, 'You killed her, you killed my mother!'

Her face contorted. 'Don't be ridiculous. I've never killed anyone.'

'Don't lie! I know you're the Vulture. I know you killed Ivo Lincoln to keep it quiet and now you're going to tell me why you killed my mother.'

I reached out, my fingers closed round the handle of a

spade and suddenly I was running at her low and hard, mesmerised by those startled eyes, that pale face and those pink lips twisted in surprise. I was almost on her when a massive pair of hands grabbed me from behind and hurled me into the bushes. I lay there, scratched and winded, looking up into Yuri's angry, upside-down face.

Grunting, he turned and began a lopsided shuffle towards Norma Craig, leg dragging, arms flailing. Maybe he wanted to get his revenge in first. If I was her I'd have been terrified but she stood her ground.

'Who are you? What do you want?'

'Don't you know me, Miss Norma?' His voice wasn't angry, it was low, almost pleading.

'Of course I don't know you. Get back and stay back.'

Yuri just kept lumbering towards her and when he was right in front of her he punched his chest and cried out. 'I am Yuri Borzov.'

Norma stayed cold and calm. 'I said, I don't know you. Now turn around, walk away and get off my property.'

Yuri flung his arm towards the lawn, tears pouring down his cheeks. 'You used to call me Harry. I work in garden, I look after pool, I mend boiler. And you, Miss Norma, you are kind to me. You say, "Harry, you should be film star."'

I'd been struggling to heave myself up but surprise snatched control of my muscles and I fell back, totally stunned. Norma let out an astonished sob and stumbled back, her eyes fixed on this ravaged mess of a man, as if, like me, she was searching for a glimpse of the good-looking boy whose chiselled features were plastered all over her photo albums.

'My God, Harry,' she breathed. 'What happened to you?'

CHAPTER 21

'I tell you everything, I lift stone from my heart,' Yuri said. He lurched back and dragged me to my feet, his bloodshot eyes wide with fury. 'You are crazy. Why you want to hurt Miss Norma? She is good woman. She is not Vulture.'

The garden door kicked open behind me and a voice that grated like steel on stone said, 'I've never liked the way that name sounds in English. Korshun has so much more of a ring to it.'

A tall, skinny woman in high heels and a fur-trimmed jacket strode in, mobile in one hand, stubby little revolver in the other. She was probably a bit older than Norma though she'd had what Mum would have called 'a lot of work' done and her skin was so stretched and mask-like it was difficult to tell her age.

'Hello, Norma,' she said. 'It's been a while.'

It was like that horrible moment in Sleeping Beauty when the wicked fairy gate crashes the christening. But after all the clues I'd got wrong and the false theories I'd chased here was the Vulture standing feet away and I didn't have a clue who she was. It looked like Norma did, though. Her quivering fingers were reaching towards the woman's face, as if she was trying to make out a dim shape trapped in a wall of ice. With a strangled moan Norma clapped her hand to her mouth and gasped, 'It's not possible . . .'

The woman said, coolly, 'A new nose, a few nips and tucks but underneath it's still me.'

Norma was staring at her, wild eyed. 'Greville . . . he killed you . . .'

'No, Norma. That was the sheer genius of it. I killed him.'

A terrible sound – half sob, half scream – spurted out of Norma's mouth.

'And actually my name isn't Janice Gribben. Never was. It's Jana Morozova.'

The shock was like a blast force ripping through reality, roaring in my ears and turning my brain to sponge. I struggled to catch hold of scraps of meaning before they sank into the mush. Janice wasn't dead. Janice was the Vulture. Janice wasn't even English. She was some crazy Russian!

Yuri made a move. Janice lifted her gun and growled at him. He stepped back.

'Don't feel bad about it Norma, everyone fell for my

dowdy English housekeeper act. That's why the KGB sent me here.'

Norma was sobbing and shaking her head like a wind-up toy. 'The KGB? You're insane. Why would the KGB send anyone to Elysium?'

'Oh, don't be so naïve – all those politicians, scientists and military brass rubbing shoulders with your wild celebrity friends. It was perfect for meeting contacts, running spies, catching the odd minister in a compromising position and making him pay for his indiscretions with a few confidential documents. It's amazing what people will do to hide their grubby little secrets. You of all people should know that, Norma.'

You could tell by the way Norma flinched that she'd caught her right where it hurt. But what with the shock of Janice rising from the dead and the struggle to see how Mum's death fitted into this chaos, Norma's secret was the last thing on my mind.

Norma's knees were giving way. As Nina stumbled out of the bushes to catch her it all kicked off. Yuri threw himself at Jana, Shrek and Bogdan burst out of the undergrowth, Shrek grabbed me, Nina jabbed him in the hand with a trowel, somewhere in the madness I heard Oz barking, and then a gun went off. The force of the shot sent Yuri spinning backwards and he fell down, clutching his arm.

'That's better,' Jana said, calmly smoothing her hair, which was blonde, stiff and about as fake as her smile. Though hatred was blurring my vision, for a split second I had the feeling I'd seen that smile before. As she turned her head it came to me. She'd been one of the summit delegates in that leaflet I'd found in Ivo Lincoln's bag.

She was studying us, like we were bits of meat on a slab and when she got to Nina she said something in Russian and curled her lip when Nina stared at her feet and nodded. Then she shifted her attention to me.

'Quite the little sleuth, aren't we, Joe Slattery? But thanks for getting Viktor Kozek involved. It saved me the bother of having to bring any more of my own people over.'

I looked away, trying to blank out her jeering words and her mocking smile. But I couldn't blank out how much I hated myself for trusting Kozek.

Things were looking bad but got a whole lot worse the minute I spotted him and the heavies from the hospital car park coming out of the house with Viktor. He had his phone out. Jana's mobile buzzed. She answered it and fixed her cold, crazy eyes on Norma. 'Sorry about your bodyguard, Norma, my colleagues have just made sure he won't be getting in my way.'

She said something into the phone in Russian. Viktor and the heavies turned right around and went back inside. Whatever it was she'd come for, she obviously didn't want Viktor listening in.

Yuri was groaning and as I bent down to help him Jana flapped her hand and snapped, 'Don't worry about him. As soon as I've got the information I need, I'll be putting you all out of your misery.'

Her tone was so matter-of-fact it took me a couple of seconds to realise what she meant. Though I s'pose I'd known from the minute she'd kicked open the door that it was going take more than a prince and a kiss to give this story a happy ending.

Norma toppled forward, sobbing, 'Why did you kill Greville, Janice, why?'

'I had to. He found out about the spy ring.'

'How?' Norma was crumbling and the sound came out like the screech of an electric saw. Nina tried to hold her up and smeared blood all down Norma's cheek. Norma didn't notice. She was in such a state she hadn't even asked who Nina was.

'Funnily enough, it was all the fault of this podgy little Venus,' Jana said. She tapped her gun against the one-armed statue, smirking at the echoey noise. 'Hear that? Hollow.' She lifted back the ivy round its legs and pointed the gun at a jagged hole where its foot should have been. 'And see that? A perfect postbox – discretely covered by ivy, hidden from general view by the greenhouse, easily accessible through the door in the wall. Ideal for exchanging messages with visiting operatives.'

Scarily, Jana Morozova wasn't coming across as a psycho murderer crowing about her crimes, more like a smug business executive. I didn't care how she said it. I just wanted her to get on with it and start talking about Nan and Mum.

She cracked her icy smile again. 'On the night of the murder I thought I had the house to myself. Clairmont was in London, you were on your way back from a photo shoot and I'd given most of the staff the night off. Just as it was getting dark I came down to the statue to leave a little package for one of our agents who'd be coming to your anniversary ball. I didn't know that Clairmont had come home early and gone round the back way, straight to the greenhouse. I don't think he'd ever set foot in there before but that day he'd bought you some fancy orchid and I suppose he wanted to keep it hot-housed overnight. There were no lights in the greenhouse and I didn't see him. Unfortunately he saw me.'

You could tell that Janice – or I s'pose I should call her Jana – was enjoying every minute of this but once she finished I promised myself I'd find a way to wipe that sick smile off her face.

'As soon as I'd gone Clairmont retrieved the package. Inside it he found some rather incriminating photographs of some very important people, the guest list for the weekend and a message written in code. He stormed into the hall and confronted me. If I hadn't killed him on the spot he'd have compromised our whole operation.' She glanced at me. Her eyes were empty – no feeling, no sympathy, no emotion in there at all – and I knew that's how she must have looked at Clairmont just before she killed him.

'How did you do it?' I breathed.

'I hit him with a vase then I snapped his neck, just to make sure he was dead. I'd been well trained. It was all very quick and clean.' She saw me screw up my face. 'It was war. All right, a cold war. But he was the enemy.'

I felt like I'd been trapped in a time warp. We'd done the Cold War in history – with proper history books full of black-and-white photos of grim-faced Russians in over-the-top uniforms, and pasty-looking Brits with moustaches and bowler hats, and here was Jana Morozova talking like it happened last week.

'He was nobody's enemy,' Norma howled. 'And when you killed him you destroyed us both. You left me with nothing! Even my memories were tainted . . .'

'Oh, do shut up, Norma, you always were a hysteric,' Jana said.

Norma's slanty eyes were two dark pits of hatred. She put a hand on Nina's shoulder and slowly heaved herself up. For a moment a flash of the feisty Norma came back. 'Why are you here . . . what do you want?' she demanded.

'I'm just tidying up a few loose ends. I've been looking for Yuri ever since he gave my people the slip in Ukraine. When I heard you were back at Elysium I thought he might get the urge to salve his conscience and throw himself on your mercy. So Viktor got Nina here's father to put the place under surveillance and, as you can see, my hunch paid off.'

Nina's chin quivered, cracking the brave mask she'd been wearing all day but Jana was having far too good a time tormenting Norma to even notice.

'What do you mean, *salve his conscience?*' Norma demanded. 'What did he have to do with any of this?'

'Don't you get it, Norma? Your handsome Harry, the gardener you thought was a penniless refugee, he was KGB, too. I brought him over to help with the dreary day-to-day tasks like dealing with people who got in my way.'

'Harry!' Norma cried. 'Tell me it's not true.'

His eyes were desperate and pleading. If this was the

confession he'd wanted to make to Norma, no wonder he'd called it a stone on his heart.

'KGB force me, Miss Norma, they threaten my family. But I did not hurt Lord Clairmont.' He stabbed a finger at Jana. 'She did that, she kill him all on her own.'

'You buried him, though, didn't you, Yuri? Out there in the woods,' Jana said.

Yuri clutched his head. 'He was good to me, he was my friend, and now every night he is there, in my dreams, covered in blood.'

'The woods,' Norma sobbed, 'Greville's poor battered body . . . buried in the woods.'

Jana flicked a fallen leaf off her sleeve. 'Oh, don't worry, he made a neat job of it, didn't you, Yuri? I made him put everything Clairmont had with him in a little tin box and bury that separately, just in case we ever needed to retrieve it. A few of his possessions turning up here and there would have been a great way to convince the world he was still alive. As it turned out, the belief that he'd gone into hiding took on a life of its own and we never needed them.'

I remembered the mud smears on Yuri's old Oxo tin, and shuddered. But at least now I knew how he'd got hold of Clairmont's tie-clip, keys and emeralds.

Norma turned her rage on Yuri. 'You told the police you saw Greville put her body in his car.'

'KGB make me say it. They make me lie to police, to everyone.'

Jana rolled her eyes. 'To be honest, Norma, I'd been worried from the start that he'd lose his nerve but fear kept him silent for years. In fact, he didn't mess up until ... ooh, it must have been fifteen years ago. Long after the KGB was disbanded and I was doing very nicely in business. Mainly oil, but some of my less . . . *official* ventures were really taking off. He was in a bar when the news came on TV – *Jana Morozova, millionaire oil magnate, awarded top job in Russian energy ministry*. According to my informants, he got drunk and started shooting his mouth off about me murdering Greville Clairmont. Well, I couldn't have that. I had an international reputation to maintain. So I had him arrested. Pathetic really. I should have had him killed then and there.'

'If only I'd known Greville was innocent,' Norma moaned. 'If only I'd known.'

'I wouldn't be telling you now if it wasn't for some nosy journalist. What was his name, Joe? Lichfield, Lancaster? *Lincoln* . . . that's right.'

I could feel Norma's eyes staring at me bewildered but I couldn't tear my concentration away from Jana for even a second to look at her.

'He found out, didn't he?' I said. 'He was going to write the story.'

'That's right, Joe. I have to say, I thought you and the Professor did rather well to work it out. Lincoln was covering a big energy summit I'm speaking at, happened to visit the KGB archive in Kiev, looked up my name and got the whole thing. My details, Yuri's details, the names of all our agents – you wouldn't believe the number of high-up Brits who were involved – my report on the murder and, of course, chapter and verse on the tabs we kept on you, Norma, just in case you ever started digging into darling Greville's disappearance and got suspicious. Lincoln thought he'd got the scoop of the century, tracked Yuri down and went running off to interview him in prison. So I had to have him silenced.'

I couldn't take it. I lunged at her, yelling, 'And you killed my mother. Why? What did she ever do to you?'

The side of her gun sent my head tipping and whirling. My vision blurred, I heard Norma screaming, 'Stop it, he's just a child!' and, in a snarling flash of white fangs, glinting eyes and flattened ears, Oz came leaping out of the bushes and sank his teeth into Jana's ankle, holding on even when she fell back screaming and kicking, trying to shake him off. In seconds Bogdan had wrenched him away and hurled him across the garden, and I was staring down the barrel of his gun.

Jana touched her leg, rubbed her bloody fingers in disbelief and hissed, 'Get inside. All of you. Now!'

I twisted away, saw Oz lying on the grass, heard a faint whimper then silence.

'Nooooo!' I was running towards him stumbling, choking, blinded. Bogdan caught my hair, yanking me back. I lashed out kicking and punching. Suddenly he let go, I fell forward, heard a click and turned. Shrek was holding Nina and he had his gun rammed against her head. She was reaching for Oz, her mouth stretched wide with horror.

'For God's sake,' Jana snarled. 'It's just a dog. Now get inside. All of you.'

Shrek let Nina go and pushed me towards the house. I

moved slowly, on jelly legs, looking back at the heap of white fur on the grass, too numb to cry.

Norma shrugged off Jana's gun. 'Why don't you just kill us all out here and have done with it?' she said.

'Too messy,' Jana said. 'This way, once I've got the information I need, there'll be a gas explosion, a terrible fire and nothing left of any of you. You know how I've always liked things tidy.'

But she was limping and underneath the sneer she was gritting her teeth.

They herded us into the sitting room and forced us to the floor with our backs to the wall. I sagged forward with my head down. I'd never felt so helpless in my life. The Vulture had taken everything I'd ever cared about and I'd been an idiot to think there was anything I could do about it. I felt Yuri's hand take mine. He squeezed it hard. I twisted my head and glanced at him. OK so he looked like a corpse and smelled like a sewer and his whole body was covered in injuries, but his eyes still gleamed defiance and I knew he hadn't given up, not yet. I pulled myself up a little. Then I squeezed that cracked leather claw right back.

In the flickering firelight Nina's pale face looked like a Hallowe'en mask. The cuts on her lip had opened up again and the purple shadows under her eyes had turned black. Jana hobbled over to the fire and helped herself to a gold-tipped cigarette from the box on the mantelpiece. Reaching for Norma's jade table lighter, she flicked the thumbwheel. It barely sparked. Annoyed, she bent and searched the crackling flames, carefully selected a glowing twig, pressed the cigarette against the ember and flopped down on the nearest couch, inhaling deeply and inspecting the teeth marks in her leg.

'Shame about the dog,' she snapped. 'I'd like to have shot it myself.'

I wanted to kill her. I jerked forward. Yuri pulled me back.

Janice flicked her hand at Norma. 'Get a first-aid kit and sort out my leg. About time you did something for me.' She signalled Bogdan to go with her. 'And hurry up.'

Shrek posted himself by the door, passing the time by pointing his gun at each of us in turn and flicking the trigger, making it crystal clear that he was really going to enjoy pulling it.

CHAPTER 22

My eyes roved the room looking for an escape route. Windows – locked. Door – guarded by a crazy gunman. Available weapons – none. Chances of survival – zip. Halfway round, my eyes met Nina's doing the same recce. I raised my wrist and quietly circled the dial of an imaginary watch. She got the message. Somehow we had to keep psycho Jana talking while we figured a way out of there.

Norma came back and got down on her knees to see to Jana's leg. Jana leant back on the cushions. 'Just like old times, eh, Norma? Only now it's *you* doing the grovelling.'

I watched Norma cutting away Jana's shredded tights and rifling through the first-aid box and wondered how much damage I could do with a pair of nail scissors and a packet of wet wipes.

'Clean it properly,' Jana snapped. 'I don't want that rancid mutt giving me blood poisoning. What's in that bottle?'

'Surgical spirit.'

'That'll do.'

Hunched in misery, Norma took a ball of cotton wool, wet it from the bottle and started dabbing at the wound.

Jana took a sharp breath, snapped her fingers and sent Nina off to the bar. She came back with a bottle of Vodka and a tumbler. Jana unscrewed the cap and poured herself a stiff drink, raising it in a mocking toast and knocking it back.

Go on, Joe, get her talking.

It was worse than chewing barbed wire but I kept my voice even. 'How come the newspapers said Clairmont mistook you for Norma? You don't look anything like her.'

'Simple. I fused the lights so it looked like he'd mistaken us in the dark.'

She reached for the vodka and I raided my memory for movies where the cornered good guy survives by knocking up a deadly weapon out of chewing gum and old toenail clippings. *Come on, Joe, think! Think! THINK!*

My eyes flicked to the bottles on the coffee table, clocking the vodka and homing in on the words 90% *alcohol* on the surgical spirit, while my mashed-up brain started throwing up scenes from old war films: tanks in war-torn ghettos, resistance fighters making Molotov cocktails, fearless kids darting through the rubble and lobbing them at the Nazis. Bottle, fuel, rag, matches. Whiz, smash, boom!

I blinked at Nina, dragged her eyes towards the bottles then across to the fire and put two fingers to my lips like a little kid pretending to smoke. She didn't get it. I tried again. Her brow wrinkled.

Jana jabbed her foot into Norma's shoulder. 'Of course, it was all down to you that I got away with it.'

'You're lying!' Norma sobbed. 'I wasn't even there.'

'That's the point. You were due back any moment and if you'd come home on time you'd have made things very difficult. As it was, Clairmont hadn't been dead more than five minutes when you called to say you'd met up with friends and wouldn't be back till late.' Jana slopped more Vodka into her glass. 'That gave me the time I needed to fake the evidence and make it look as if he'd murdered me and gone on the run.'

Norma, who was already a quivering mess, lost it completely and fell forward, crying, 'No, no, no …'

'What about the forensics?' I said. 'How come the cops never worked out that you were the murderer?' I wasn't even playing for time. I really wanted to know.

Jana laughed. 'Back then, forensic testing wasn't nearly so advanced. All I had to do was make the murder scene look right.'

'How? How did you do it?' Nina croaked.

Jana looked almost gratified that we were so interested. 'First, I opened a vein in my arm and collected some of my own blood. Then I washed the vase I'd used to kill Clairmont and smeared it with my blood and hair, to make it look as if he'd grabbed the nearest object and smashed me over the head in a moment of fury. Then I splashed some more of my blood around the hall, dropped one of my shoes in the mess, put on Clairmont's shoes and laid a trail of his bloody footprints out to his Mercedes. Once I'd checked that Yuri had buried the body and briefed him on what he should tell the police, I packed a bag, drove Clairmont's Mercedes to Dover and left it on the cliff top with a few more of my hairs, some fibres from my housekeeper's uniform and my other blood-stained shoe in the boot. After that, a rather fetching black wig, a fake passport and the early-morning ferry to France got me out of England undetected. Just before boarding I called the police anonymously, telling them that a man fitting Clairmont's description had been seen throwing a body over the cliffs at Dover. The tip-off led them to his abandoned Merc, corroborated Yuri's statement that he'd seen Clairmont put Janice's body in the car, and allayed any doubts about who was the murderer and who was the victim.' She pushed her mask of a face close to Norma's and hissed, 'Genius, don't you think, Norma?'

Then she sat back, sighing. 'Of course, Yuri didn't see it that way and at first he kicked up a fuss and refused to help me. But he had no choice.' Jana sneered at him as if he was a dribble of cat sick. 'Look at him. He was no match for Jana Morozova. Not then. Not now.'

'Morozov,' I said, looking straight at Nina and then at the bottles on the table.

Jana glared at me. 'Morozova. And it's Miss Morozova to you.'

'Sorry. It's just the name, Morozov – isn't that some kind of cocktail?'

'Cocktail? What are you talking about, you idiot?'

'Maybe I got it wrong,' I mumbled, keeping my eyes fixed on Nina. 'Maybe it just *sounds* like Morozov.'

Nina's lip twitched. She'd got it. I checked the coffee table, weighing up my chances of getting to those bottles faster than Shrek or Bogdan could pull a trigger. The odds weren't encouraging.

Norma finished tying off the bandage, flinching as Jana caught her by the chin and jerked her face up. 'And you and Clairmont being such big *celebrities* really helped to keep the media spotlight off Janice. What self-respecting paper was going to devote space to a mousey little house-keeper when there was a homicidal aristocrat and a crazy supermodel to write about?'

Norma was kind of living up to that description, rocking on her knees with her eyes half closed, murmuring, 'He loved me . . . he loved me . . .' which didn't exactly fill me with hope that she was secretly plotting some miracle method of getting us out of there.

I was scrabbling for something, anything, to keep Jana talking when Nina piped up.

'Why did you not take those files out of KGB archives as soon as they were opened to public?'

Jana looked up. 'Oh, don't worry. I *sanitised* the main Moscow archive years ago.' She tipped her glass towards Yuri. 'But because *he's* Ukrainian, the KGB in Kiev had copies of everything relating to the Elysium operation. Stupid of me. If I'd realised sooner I wouldn't be here

237

now, clearing up this mess. Still it won't take long. I just need the names of everyone who knew about Lincoln's investigation, then I'll be on my way. Well, Joe? Apart from Nina and Professor Lincoln, who I'm assured won't ever regain consciousness, who did you tell?'

I looked her square in the eye. 'No one.'

She sighed and muttered to Shrek who slipped his gun down the back of his trousers and came towards me, eyes dead, hands twitchy.

I backed up. 'No one. I swear.'

She barked something in Russian. He yanked me to my feet and wrenched my arm back, locking my elbow on the point of breaking. Pain worse than anything you can imagine sawed nerves I never even knew I had. I couldn't move forward or back. I couldn't bend, breathe or even yell without ratcheting up the torment. Out of the corner of my eye I caught the glint of steel in Shrek's hand and heard a scream, only it wasn't me. It was Norma rushing towards me. Bogdan whacked her with his gun. She tottered backwards saying over and over, 'The boy has nobody. Who was he going to tell?'

Jana stood up, flexing her bandaged ankle. 'That's what we're here to find out.'

'Don't do this, Janice,' Norma pleaded. 'Let him go. I swear to God we'll keep your secret.'

'Sorry, Norma. I have to finish this tonight.'

'Why now?' Norma sobbed. 'After all these years.'

'Because of this summit I'm off to tomorrow. I'm all set to sign a huge Arctic oil contract with the British government that'll net my companies millions.'

'So sign your damn contract and leave us alone.'

'Do be sensible, Norma. I have to plug every possible leak before I get there. Can you imagine the Brits signing a deal with the woman who murdered Greville Clairmont?'

Norma crumpled into a heap of misery. Nina flashed me a look, crawled over to her, threw her arms round her neck and started blubbing into her hair. Startled at first, Norma began to rock her gently, murmuring and patting her like a little kid. Slowly, as Nina's whispers sank in, Norma's swollen eyes lifted and met mine.

Jana took a couple of careful steps to the mantelpiece and got herself another cigarette. 'Come on, Joe. Who did you tell?'

'Just the Professor,' I whimpered, petrified I'd crack and let on about Bailey. I knew I was weeping but the pain was so bad I couldn't stop.

A twitch of Shrek's fingers fired agony up my arm and jolted a scream from my lungs. The room tilted as the tip of his knife slit the flesh of my ear.

'No one else. I swear.'

His knife slid deeper. I could feel something warm and sticky dripping down my neck. My body was a twitching mess but my brain was working overtime, warning me that my plan, what there was of it, could go either way. I could deal with that. But I wasn't going to die without getting the truth about Mum.

'Why did you kill my mother?' I gasped. 'What did she have to do with any of this?'

Jana's lips peeled back. 'What do you think, Norma?

You're all about to die. Maybe it's only fair he should know.'

My heart stuttered to a stop. Jana was getting a real kick out of dragging this out but if she gave me an answer I didn't care how much she sneered. I held my breath, waiting, hoping . . . horrified. She was bending down to the fire, searching for a twig to light her cigarette. Nina tensed. This was it. Our only chance. I had to act now. But if I did I'd never find out the truth about Mum. I looked at Nina and Norma and I knew I didn't have a choice. Ignoring the burning hunger for answers and the sickening stab of pain, I opened my mouth, yelled, 'Bogdan!' and brought my knee up hard into Shrek's groin.

Startled, Bogdan swung round just as Shrek let go of me, dropped the knife and folded forward with a breathy grunt.

Nina and Norma sprang apart. Faster than a spitting snake, Nina grabbed the surgical spirit and squirted it over Jana's shoulder into the flames while Norma smashed open the vodka bottle and threw the contents down Jana's clothes.

A white hot jet of flame whooshed out of the fireplace straight into Jana's face, catching her lacquered hair and sweeping a line of blue flickers down her front. She leapt back, screaming and batting wildly at the flames. Within seconds her whole suit was alight, filling the room with the stench of burning hair and clothes. Rolling and kicking, she fell to the ground.

Bogdan panicked and rushed forward, waving his gun around but even he couldn't see how shooting anyone was going to help Jana. He dropped the weapon, leapt across the sofa, kicked aside the coffee table, and tried to roll her up in the rug. As Shrek scrambled forward to help him, Yuri grabbed his leg, tipping him over. Shrek crashed down, smashing his head against the table, adding the punch of breaking glass to the gruesome sound of Jana's shrieks. Bogdan turned, saw me grab the gun from the back of Shrek's trousers and made a dash for his own. As I fumbled with the weapon, trying to pull back the hammer, Nina hurled herself over the sofa and slithered towards Bogdan's gun, shouting to Norma who jumped on his back, clawing at his throat. He bucked and twisted, elbowing her so hard she hit the wall with a dull slap. He skirted the sofa and seized Nina's hair, ripping her head back as she grabbed the gun. She doubled over, clasping the weapon as he wrestled her down and tore at her arms till the gun tumbled free and slid across the floor. He threw himself after it, grabbed it and swerved round on his knees to take aim.

My muscles seized up, halted by the ugly, unnatural weight of the weapon in my hand, the ordinariness of the sweat on Bogdan's lip and the lock of oily hair falling across his eyes. *You have to do this, Joe, you have to*. Sick and scared I raised Shrek's gun and held it with both hands, mirroring Bogdan's grasp on his. A shot cracked through Jana's screams. I saw Nina, Yuri and Norma reach out to me in silent slo-mo, mouths opening, faces warping, and the room turned so wobbly that my body had to sway to stay upright. It was only when I looked down that I saw a crimson spurt of blood spreading across my chest. And when I looked up I saw Bogdan taking aim to fire a second shot.

CHAPTER 23

Like a sleepwalker, I watched the floor floating gently towards me. I knew I'd entered some kind of weird zone where anything could happen but I was still amazed when the door flew open and Jackson Duval burst in wielding a garden spade and cracked it across the back of Bogdan's head. The ringing crunch of metal on skull was the last thing I heard before the floor turned black and soft and sucked me into silence for what seemed like forever. Then a voice broke through, like someone speaking under water.

'Hey, Joe.'

I forced my eyes open. A face swam into focus. I could tell I was still in weird zone because it was Bailey, staring down at me through his grubby glasses. Behind him there was movement and shouting; two cops handcuffing

Viktor Kozek, a load more cops coming through the French windows, and Norma and Nina crawling towards me across the broken glass. I tried to speak. The darkness swept me away.

I was gazing into a pair of square, unblinking eyes and it took me a while to work out that they weren't eyes at all but metal lights in a plain white ceiling and all around me soft beeps, whooshing doors, faint voices and the sharp tang of disinfectant were triggering thoughts of the night Mum died and the search for answers that had been the only thing keeping me going ever since. Then it all flooded back, the night at Elysium, the world-stopping moment when Jana Morozova had been about to tell me why she'd had Mum killed and the choice I'd made. It had been the right one, I was sure of that. Only now I'd be spending the rest of my life with a big black question mark scrawled across every memory of Mum I had. That didn't seem much like a life worth living, 'specially without Oz in it, or a home to go to.

I tried to sit up, the room spun, and a woman bent over me, sploshing fat tears on to my face and whispering, 'Joe, thank God, thank God.'

Seeing as one of my hands was wired to a drip and she was holding the other one really tight, I couldn't push her away. I stared up at her, a bit bewildered, mostly embarrassed. You see, the woman doing the crying was Norma Craig.

My throat felt like sandpaper but I gave my voice a try. 'Miss . . . Craig.' I didn't sound like me, but then I didn't feel much like me either.

She poured me a cup of water and helped me take a drink.

'Is Yuri . . . all right?' I croaked. 'And . . . Nina?'

'Yuri's doing fine and they're letting Nina out tomorrow.'

The relief cut through some of the fug in my head. 'What … happened? It was like I was … hallucinating. I thought I saw these … people I know from … London.'

'You weren't hallucinating, Joe. If it hadn't been for Jackson and Bailey Duval we'd all be dead.'

'But … how …?'

'It's a little complicated. I have to say, the story gets longer every time Bailey tells it, but I can give you the gist.'

Norma hanging out with Bailey? I was back in weird zone. She sat down on the bed and I gazed at her, wondering what was coming.

'As soon as Jackson realised Viktor Kozek was tearing London apart looking for you and Yuri he decided to take Rikki and Bailey away from the estate to somewhere safe. He'd fetched Rikki from his girlfriend's mother's and was on his way back to get Bailey when Kozek and his thugs arrived and forced them up to what I understand is a penthouse flat that Jackson has converted into offices.'

Penthouse! I bit back the urge to laugh. She thought I was coughing and gave me another drink.

'When Kozek's thugs threatened Rikki, Jackson had no choice. He told them you were in Catford and handed over his phone so that Kozek could contact you and pretend to be him. Then they kept him and Rikki under guard until Viktor had picked you and Nina up.'

The fug was starting to lift. 'OK, but how come Jackson and Bailey were at Elysium?'

'That was all down to Bailey. He saw Kozek hustling Jackson and Rikki up to Jackson's office, guessed what was happening and tried to warn you. The only reply he got was your text about Balfour and Ebenezer. He was mystified, Googled the two names and up popped the Wikipedia entry for *Kidnapped*.' She raised a neat eyebrow. 'Smart thinking, Joe. I was impressed. 'However he had no real evidence, and given that Yuri was walking around with the Clairmont emeralds, Nina and her father were illegal immigrants working for a known criminal and Jackson . . . well . . .' She stopped, flustered.

'Wasn't up for any citizen of the year awards?' I suggested.

She smiled and nodded. 'For all those reasons Bailey was reluctant to contact the police. Instead he spent the next couple of hours going over every scrap of evidence the two of you had gathered and came to the conclusion that the Vulture either had to be me, or someone who had worked for me. As a form of insurance he emailed all the evidence to Keith Treadwell and as soon as Kozek's people released Jackson, Bailey made him drive him down to Elysium to confront me about your abduction. When they got there they saw Kozek's cars in the woods. So they slipped in through the back gate where Jackson armed himself with my garden spade. Then they crept up to the house, saw Viktor and a couple of thugs playing cards in the kitchen, with Raoul trussed up on the floor beside them, and managed to get a glimpse of what was happening to us in the sitting room. At that point Bailey insisted on calling 999. But things were moving fast and when Bogdan took a shot at you, Jackson ran to the rescue and knocked him out. The police arrived a few minutes later and while they dealt with Kozek and his mob you, Yuri and Nina were rushed to hospital.

'What about . . . Jana Morozova?' Just saying her name made me feel hot, and sick.

'She survived. She's in a specialist burns unit in London.'

I threw back the bedclothes and swung my legs on to the floor. Pain cracked through my chest and the room lurched the other way. I reached out to steady myself. 'I want to see her. I've got to make her tell me why she killed Mum.'

'Shhh. Get back into bed. You don't need to talk to Jana Morozova.'

'You don't understand . . .'

'I can tell you why she ordered Sadie's death.'

'You?' I looked round at her. 'How do you know?'

She hung her head. 'This isn't easy for me, Joe. I want you to promise to let me finish before you say anything at all.'

'O . . . K . . .' Mystified, I sank back on to the pillow. Norma seemed to be bracing herself to tell me something earth-shattering. A cold kind of dread crept through my body, numbing the pain in my chest. What if she was about to tell me that Mum had been leading a secret life?

What if Mum and this mysterious Lizzie had been involved in some terrible crime?

'When Greville disappeared I should have had faith in him and devoted my life to proving his innocence,' she said. 'But I didn't. I went running off to a clinic in Switzerland, convinced I'd never recover from the heart-break.' She clutched the end of the bed so tightly I thought she was going to snap the bars. 'But the thing was, Joe, I was pregnant.'

I opened my mouth to tell her I didn't want to hear about this right now. She raised her hand to stop me.

'You promised to let me finish,' she said. 'I remember sitting there, staring at those cold white mountains, hating Greville for what he'd done and gripped by the terrible fear that I'd never be able to give his baby the love it deserved or shield it from the shadow of his crime. I made a terrible decision. One I'll regret till the day I die. I decided to give my baby away. Not to strangers but to a couple I knew who were desperate for another child.' She looked right at me. 'That couple were Pam and Les Slattery. Sadie Slattery was my daughter. Her father was Greville Clairmont.'

My knees shook softly and gently detached themselves from the rest of my body. Norma was spilling words out so fast that my stupefied brain could hardly keep up.

'The only person I'd told about the pregnancy was Janice. The thought of her reporting my secret back to the KGB, keeping tabs on me, making sure I swallowed the lies about Greville makes me sick. Imagine how thrilled she must have been when I gave Sadie up.' Norma was pale and trembling, and her face was covered in a thin layer of sweat. 'I'm convinced that Ivo Lincoln discovered the details of Sadie's birth and adoption in the KGB files. Then he tracked her down to tell her the truth about her identity and the murder at Elysium, probably so he could include her story in the expose he was writing. That's why Jana Morozova had them both killed. So yes, when you turned on me in the garden and accused me of killing Sadie, in a way you were right. If I'd never given her up she'd still be alive.'

It took me a while to find any voice at all and when I did, all that came out was a croaky whimper. 'Not Lizzie. It wasn't Lizzie.'

Norma must have thought the shock had tipped my over the edge because she reached for the oxygen mask and started telling me to breathe.

I shook her off. 'When they cut Mum out of the wreckage they thought she was saying "*Tell Joe and Lizzie.*" But she wasn't. Don't you see? She was saying, "*Tell Joe, Elysium.*" She'd just found out the truth and she was desperate for me to know it, too.'

The last piece of the puzzle had snapped into place, completing a picture that was so distorted it was like catching my crazy, mangled-up reflection in a fairground mirror and finding out it was the way I really looked. I wasn't Joe Slattery. I was some weird version of him, stuck in a freaky, warped world I didn't understand. Norma was still talking and I was glad, because when she finished, then what?

'When my lawyer told me Sadie had died and you

were living in Saxted, I felt an overwhelming need to see you and to tell you my secret. That's why I came back to England and that's why I arranged that ridiculous charade with the food deliveries. But when you walked into Elysium that first evening I saw Greville's face in yours, the same eyes, the way you stood. And then, at the very end, when you smiled at me, just the way he used to … I couldn't deal with it. I still believed he was a killer and all the old fears welled up. I kept asking myself, were you better off not knowing the truth about your grandfather? Had you inherited the twisted genes that made him a murderer?' She gazed at me, her eyes pleading and full of tears. 'And now that we know he was innocent, can you ever forgive me for abandoning Sadie?'

A bit of me wanted to hate her for what she'd done to Mum, another bit could see she hated herself enough for the both of us, and the rest of me was still recovering from the shock of finding out her secret.

'I . . . I don't know . . .' I said.

Right then all I wanted to do was get away from her and her questions because I had a couple of my own crying out to be answered, the main ones being, *Who am I?* and *What's going to happen to me now?* The voices in my head were screaming *What now?* so loudly I almost missed Norma saying, 'I want the truth to come out, Joe. I want the world to know you are my grandson and, if you agree, I'll ask my lawyers to have you recognised as Lord Joel Clairmont, eighth Earl of Rutherford.'

My mouth made shapes but there wasn't any sound coming out.

She squeezed her hands, nervously. 'And I hope very much that you will come to live with me at Elysium.'

The screaming in my head went silent because I guess she'd kind of answered my questions.

I was still trying to get my head round the idea that this rich, famous woman was Mum's real mum, when I realised that I was in a posh, private room, not a ward, and that Norma must be paying for it. There were comfy armchairs for visitors, a basket of fruit by the bed and a big vase of flowers on the windowsill. I stared at the flowers. They were white rosebuds.

'Was it you who put that big white wreath on Mum's grave?' I said.

She blinked in surprise. 'Yes. Yes, it was. I was horrified when it got vandalised.'

'It wasn't vandals that trashed it. It was me.'

She pulled back. 'Joe! Whatever possessed you?'

'I thought the Vulture had sent them . . . gloating about killing her.'

'Oh, Joe.' Norma's face contorted and she started doing this strange laughing-crying thing. 'I've had enough of lies and misunderstandings. Let's choose the next lot of flowers for Sadie together. And while we're about it we'll pick out a headstone.'

I hesitated.

'Please, Joe,' she said. 'Let me at least do that for her.'

'Yeah, OK.' A lump turned slowly in my stomach. 'And I want to give Oz a proper send-off. Bury him somewhere in the garden at Elysium and put a marker on the grave or plant a tree or something.'

She wiped her eyes and frowned. 'I don't think that would be a good idea.'

'What's the problem? Lots of people do it!'

'The problem is, Joe, Oz isn't dead. The vet said he might end up with a bit of a limp. But he should be fine for a good few years yet.'

It was my turn to do that laughing-crying thing and for a while I couldn't stop. I had answers, I had Oz, I had somewhere to live and maybe one day I'd find a way to forgive Norma for giving Mum away.

CHAPTER 24

It was Norma's idea to throw a party at Elysium to celebrate my release from hospital. She thought it would bring us together and help me settle in. I wasn't so sure about that but in the end I agreed, on condition it was nothing like the parties she used to throw in that house.

For a start, her 'Only the beautiful' policy had to go. It would have kept half the guests I wanted to invite right off the list and I didn't want a buffet or any poncey ice sculptures. I wanted a barbeque, with proper food, like ribs and steaks and burgers. Surprisingly she'd been well up for that but insisted on having gold-edged invites printed that said '*The Dowager Lady Rutherford*' – that's what she calls herself now — '*and Lord Joel Clairmont*' – that's me, weird huh? – '*at Home.*'

I said to her, who'd be dumb enough to invite people

253

round when they *weren't* going to be home but she said that's what you put on invites if you're a lord. I didn't get it. But there's a whole bunch of stuff I don't get, now I've acceded to the title. *Acceded* – I hear that word all the time these days, even use it sometimes, though I still have trouble believing it was me who did the acceding.

Take it from me, there's just no way of knowing how people are going to react when they find out you're a lord. Then again, perhaps I shouldn't have just sprung it on them when they turned up at the hospital. Bailey laughed so much that Nina had to haul him outside because just looking at me kept setting him off. George, on the other hand, took it pretty calmly, maybe because Doreen started having some kind of fit, only unlike Bailey's it wasn't a laughing one.

Still, I couldn't have cared less what Doreen thought about anything and Bailey was welcome to take the mick as much as he wanted, seeing as he was the one who'd 'saved my hide' as he called it. Norma was right, though; his side of the story did get longer every time he told it (which was a lot) and when he got to the bit about my coded *Kidnapped* text you'd think *he'd* been the Einstein for doing a bit of Googling.

Trouble was, getting the police involved had made things sticky for Yuri and even stickier for Nina's dad. But Norma's lawyer, Angus Pritchard, had got them out on bail and, seeing as they'd both been forced to commit their crimes and were key witnesses in the case that Scotland Yard was building against Viktor Kozek, Pritchard thought there was decent chance of them getting reduced or even suspended sentences. Unlike Viktor, Shrek, Bogdan and the rest of Kozek's mob who'd all be going down for a very long time.

Jana Morozova was still in a specialist burns unit but, believe it or not, she was getting off scot free. And as soon as they could move her they were sending her back to Russia. I know, it makes me puke. Some minister came round to see Norma, claiming that the government's hands were tied because of Jana's diplomatic immunity. But if you ask me she'd cut a deal – her freedom in exchange for keeping quiet about all the Brits in high places who'd spent the sixties and seventies helping out the KGB. Still, as Norma said, with injuries like Jana Morozova's she wouldn't be living much of life, and I can't say I was sorry.

Course, the minute it got out about Clairmont being a victim not a murderer and me being a lord, the papers went crazy and all these paparazzi camped out in the woods and hid in the trees, snapping photos of me and Norma on long-lens cameras. In the end Norma gave up on her bid for privacy and called a press conference. The reporters lapped it up, 'specially when she posed for their cameras and flashed them her million-dollar smile. I looked a right prat in the photos they took of us together but no one seemed to care.

A couple of days later we had a private burial for Greville Clairmont in the Clairmont family crypt at Saxted church. It was the total opposite of the memorial service they held for him in London, which was all over the TV news with wall-to-wall barefaced liars crawling out of the woodwork, claiming they'd never doubted his innocence for a minute.

As for the Clairmont emeralds, well, it turned out that Yuri *had* sold the earrings to Fat Marty (for a measly fifty quid) before getting out of Catford fast. Then Fat Marty had tried to get the stones recut and that's when the rumours about the Clairmont emeralds had started flying round the black market. Anyway, I took Norma round to see Fat Marty and she managed to buy the earrings back 'no questions asked'. But that slimy creep still charged her five hundred quid for the privilege.

Elysium looked totally different with all the curtains open, the sunshine turning the glass front into a sparkling, sky-filled mirror and the lawns mowed to a stripy rolling velvet. In a red silk shirt, white trousers and that new short swishy hairdo she called a 'bob', Norma was barely recognisable as the weirdo woman in black I'd met all those weeks ago, and you could see she was just loving the chance to work her famous hostess magic again. It took her about two seconds to get Albert Brewster, the St Saviour's porter, swapping stories with some of her celebrity mates from way back, Mum's friend Shauna having a laugh with the vicar of Saxted, and Bitsy Lincoln chatting away to one of my Clairmont cousins, who was called Francesca. This Francesca had an uncanny look of Mum about her, 'specially when she laughed, and when I finally plucked up the nerve to go over and talk to her she turned out be musical, too. Only she played the violin in some orchestra and said she couldn't sing a note.

But even the new palm trees, huge yellow umbrellas and hoards of waiters running up and down, couldn't stop the pool area looking more like a WWI field hospital than a swanky sun terrace. There was Yuri laid out on a sun lounger resting his busted arm and leg, Raoul with a dirty great bandage round his head, Prof Lincoln in a wheelchair with a walking stick at his side, me with my chest and arm strapped up and Oz with one of those lampshade things round his neck to stop him biting his stitches. Everyone was pretty cheerful though, 'specially Yuri who kept singing sentimental songs in Russian, downing Vodkas and toasting everything in sight. Raoul was still having trouble getting used to me and Oz moving in, though he got his revenge by calling me my 'my lord' really loudly whenever Bailey was around.

Bailey was staying with us for a few days because Norma thought the country air would help his asthma. It seemed to be working. He was over by the gazebo looking healthier than I'd seen him for ages and chatting with his new best mate Keith Treadwell and some famous photographer from Norma's modelling days, who'd flown in from LA.

The pool was twinkly, turquoise and heated to the perfect temperature. Jackson was sitting on the edge, dangling Rikki in the shallow end while Danielle did lazy lengths in a white bikini and tried to ignore Oz, who was barking at her from the side.

'Oz, be quiet. Here you go!' I slid the sausage out of my hot dog and chucked it at him. He gulped it down and started barking again. Now that we were living at Elysium he'd come round to country life big time. Massive grounds to run around in, endless statues to pee against, a comfy bed in a warm kitchen with the option of the couches in the sitting room for general day-time lounging and flea scratching. Doggy heaven. I was the one who still couldn't believe that we were here to stay.

Jackson glanced up. I couldn't see his eyes, just my own face reflected in his shades.

'Hey, Joe.' He flicked his head towards a nearby sun lounger.

'Hey, Jackson.' I sat down nervously. I'd seen him a couple of times since the night he saved my life but not to talk to on his own, and I had a horrible feeling he was about to have a go at me for 'bringing those crazy Ukes down on all our heads'. I s'pose I couldn't have blamed him if he had.

'I'm sorry I disobeyed you, Jackson, I never thought that—'

'You did what you had to do, Joe. I respect that.' He pulled Rikki out of the water and started drying him off. 'And you got to respect that I did what I had to do, giving you up to Kozek.'

'I do, totally.'

'It wasn't nothing personal. You're family.' He pulled a T-shirt over Rikki's head. 'But when you got a kid, that kid got to come first. That's just how it is.'

Norma was watching us from the top of the steps and when he said that I thought for a moment she was going to cry. But she just sniffed a bit and said that Rikki was very lucky to have a dad like Jackson. Then she looked at me and I knew we were both imagining how things might have turned out if she'd put Mum first.

A screech of feedback signalled the start of the music and jolted us back to the party. Oh, I forgot to mention that I'd got Ronan Bellfield's band along — remember him? He was the busker who saved me from starvation when I took Nina into A and E. 'Course, having his band there was nothing compared to the last party Norma threw at Elysium when the Rolling Stones turned up and played all night. But I'd lent Ronan some of Mum's tapes and when he sang a couple of her songs I saw Norma standing there, transfixed by the sound. She said it was the kind of stuff Greville Clairmont had really loved — and he'd never liked the Stones much anyway.

Nina was leaning against the stage, watching as people started dancing. She'd done something radical to her hair — brushed it maybe — and she looked all right in her new blue dress, though in my mind I'd always see her in scraggy jeans with a dirty old hat pulled right down or frowning at me in the moonlight telling me, 'That is not plan.'

I went over to her, fished out the little box I'd been carrying around all day and pushed it into her hand. 'I got this for you,' I said.

'For me?' Embarrassed, she twisted away to open it and then turned back, holding up the gold chain Norma had helped me pick out, and gazing at the dangling pendant hanging off it. It was a diamond clamped between two prancing bears and it glinted in the sunshine as she fastened it round her neck.

Neither of us said anything, just stood there, remembering the nightmare we'd shared and looking at each other like no one else existed. For the first time ever I saw her well up and I knew I'd rather die than let anyone hurt her again.

'Hey, what's that?' Bailey said, barging between us and reaching for the pendant.

'I got it made from the tie-clip that saved us,' I said.

He pulled a face. 'I s'pose it looks better than hanging my laptop round her neck.'

'Yeah, all right,' I said. 'The tie-clip that *helped* save us.'

Nina smiled at Bailey. 'I will not take chances. Next time I meet with Joe I will bring Swiss army knife and leave phone on so you can hear everything that happens.'

Bailey did a fake shudder. 'Er . . . no thanks.'

'Who is that?' Nina said, pointing to a tall, skinny kid, heading towards us across the grass.

I squinted into the sunlight. I couldn't believe it. It was Horse Boy! I'd just started telling them about the time he fell off his horse and called me a chav, when he came right up and elbowed Bailey and Nina out of the way, as if they weren't even worth noticing. Then he started grinning and pumping my hand, like he'd just given me a school prize.

'Hello, I'm Hugo Talbot-French. I didn't get a chance to introduce myself last time we met.' *No, Hugo, you were too busy giving me the finger.* I caught Bailey mimicking him behind his back and tried not to laugh. 'My parents own the equestrian centre on the other side of the village. As soon as you're out of those bandages we were wondering if you'd like to come over for a ride and a bite of lunch.'

For a couple of seconds I was too gobsmacked to speak. But I managed to force something out. 'Thanks all the same. But me and Oz'll leave horse riding to *civilised* people.'

That rattled him, but it was nothing compared to the panic and bewilderment on his face when Bailey started swinging his head and shoulders in opposite directions, put on a heavy street voice and said, 'Yo fam, yeah, that's calm. I'll come tho'. Man's always wanted to do a bita hoss ridin' and that still! Tomoro cool, yeah?'

But Hugo had picked up enough of it to get the message that he'd be taking Bailey riding in the morning. I had to walk away or I'd have cracked up and burst my stitches.

I sidled up to Doreen who was perched on the edge of a deckchair, watching George and the St Saviour's cox debating Cambridge's chances in the next boat race.

'So . . . how's it going, Doreen?' I said.

She glanced up at me, stiff-lipped under her floppy pink hat, and said, 'My father spoiled Sadie rotten, right up until the day he died.' Though it was more to herself than to me and her voice was a bit slurred. 'My little duchess, he used to called her. And now I know why. I never felt a connection to her, not from the minute she arrived, but all I ever heard was "Come on, Doreen, be nice to your little sister," like she was the only person in the house who mattered.'

She looked so miserable, I almost felt sorry for her.

She downed her wine and grabbed another from a passing waiter. 'But then we only *had* a house because of her.'

'What do you mean?'

'Norma Craig's lawyer just told me. It was Norma who gave my parents Laurel Cottage. A gift for taking her child and keeping her secret. How was I supposed to compete with that?'

I didn't have an answer and I turned to go.

'But I'll say one thing for Sadie,' she said.

I stopped.

'Once she'd set her heart on something she wouldn't give up, even when the chances of it working out were impossible.' I swivelled round to look at her. 'Looks like you're built the same way.'

'Yeah, looks like I am,' I said, which is probably the nearest that me and Doreen would ever get to a normal conversation.

I slipped away to get a burger, relishing the sting of mustard on my lips, which proved that this really was my life, not some wacky reality show where the producers threw a pool party for the randomest mix of people they could find. The band started up the intro to another of Mum's songs and I caught myself searching the crowd as if I'd see her heading for the stage.

I felt a hand on my shoulder. It was Norma.

'What are you thinking?' she said.

'That Mum should be here.'

'I know,' she said, quietly.

She wanted me to ease her pain and tell her I forgave her. I felt bad that the best I could come up with was, 'You gave her to good people who loved her.'

'That was the only thing I ever did for her, Joe. And now

I'll never be able to make it up to her.'

The music stopped. I looked up. Yuri had commandeered the microphone and he was leaning on one crutch, pulling out a piece of paper. Little waves of nudging and shushing rippled across the garden as he coughed loudly and started to read.

'For last thirty-six years I dream of day when dark past of Elysium will end and bright future of Elysium will begin. And now, because of my brave friend Joe, that day is come. His grandfather was good man and Joe is good boy.' Swapping the paper for a glass of vodka he raised it high. 'So now we drink toast to Joe and Elysium!'

The cries of 'Joe! Elysium!' caught me off guard, ripping the familiar stab of misery through my guts. I stood there among the smiles and clinking glasses, feeling Mum's frustration as she'd struggled to gasp out the truth she'd wanted me to know. *Tell Joe, Elysium.* I squeezed my fists, ready for the rush of falling helplessness that always followed the bursts of pain.

It didn't come. I unclenched my fists and felt my fingers reaching for Norma's hand.

There is something else you did for Mum,' I said. 'Something really important.'

Norma looked at me with a sad smile. 'Really, Joe? What was that?'

'You fulfilled her dying wish,' I said. 'You told me who I am.'

ACKNOWLEDGEMENTS

Many thanks to Sarah Curtis, Beth Holgate, Kevin Loader, Jamie Buxton and Catherine Saunders for their helpful feedback on an early draft, Ariadne Arendt and Minty Barnor for help with translations, and John Tullett for advice on how to hotwire a car. I would also like to thank my wonderful agent Stephanie Thwaites at Curtis Brown for her support, enthusiasm and clever input, and my editor Rachel Leyshon for her clear eye, firm guidance and brilliant suggestions. And of course a big thank you to my children Charlotte, Murdo and Lily for helping me to get into Joe's head, and to my husband James for everything.

ABOUT THE AUTHOR

Sam Hepburn read modern languages at Cambridge University and worked for many years as a documentary maker for the BBC. She lives in London with her husband and three children.

www.samhepburnbooks.com
www.samosmanbooks.com